Scared of Loving You

India Norfleet

Dedication

This book is dedicated to all of those who are scared to love but courageously does so anyway!!

Acknowledgements

I've done it again! This is book number thirteen and I still can't believe I'm living my childhood dream! I've grown so much as an author and person since my first book and it just feels amazing! I can't wait to see where I'll be five years from now...I keep trying to picture it but I know that my image won't compare to the many blessings Jesus has in store for me. There is no way that I would still be doing what I love if it was not for our Lord and Savior Jesus Christ. I didn't know just how blessed I am to be living my dreams until I actually thought about just how many people that had come and told me that they were consumed with regret for not following theirs.

I was so scared when I first began my writing journey, kept thinking that I would fail, kept doubting myself...but then one day I took a deep breath and stepped out on faith and let me tell you it was I've been flying ever since. Jesus is real, awesome, amazing and as imperfect as I am, still loves me unconditionally. A little faith will carry you a mighty long way, if only you just believe in yourself and the power of the All Mighty.

To my husband, the love of my life, my heart and number one fan, De'Francis Lewis. I love you more than life itself. Thank you so much for believing in me when I didn't believe in myself. To both of my babies Niya and Dre, thank you for showing mommy the only definition of unconditional love. My heart has no beat without you two. Mommy, Norvis Whitfield, I love you so much; I don't know where I would be without your love. Thank you for loving me so much and always believing in every dream I've ever had. To my daddy and stepmom, Karl and Cricket Norfleet, the look of pride in your eyes whenever you tell me how proud of me you are is priceless. I love both of you so much. Tieste Flynn, I couldn't ask for a better sister and friend than you.

To my mother and father-in-law, as well as sisters-in-laws, Elvira and Andre Lewis, Argentina Abney, and Deliccia Anderson, you all are so good to me and have always had my back no matter the situation. I love you all with every beat of my heart. Heather Carter, I couldn't ask for a better publicist and friend. Ever since I've become your client, you've had nothing but my best interest at heart. Thank you from the bottom of my heart. Cora Hawkins, the world's best photographer and my sister from another mother, I love you so much. I don't know what I'd do without you.

To Danielle Marcus the CEO of Danielle Marcus Presents and to the rest of the DMP family thanks so much for welcoming me to the family and showing me so much love and support.

To my Detroit Author Alliance family, you all continue to hold me down and standing in my corner no matter what. You all came into my life right on time, inspiring, encouraging, and teaching all at the same time. What I've found with you guys is a place to belong, an anchor of support through the good and difficult times, and most importantly a home. King Benjamin, Lakelia Bird Deloach, Danielle Marcus, and Kenya Rivers, I am tremendously grateful to have you all in my life. DAA 4 life - LOL. I love you guys!

And to my awesome family and support system: TameshaDeason , TilyneStorey, Shayna Phillips, ShakyraChaneyfield, ShantaLunn, Sherita Smith,

Latonya Clayton, Delorian Ross, Delonda Rushing, Natasha Decker, Tara Jackson-Clark, De'Sean Mays, Karlsterling Norfleet, Deanna King (my awesome makeup artist), Yolanda Sims, Tiffany Haley,Sharee Rompf, Shantina Robinson, Ryshanda Henderson, James Stokes, Krystal Carter, Cindy Robinson, Melissa Johnson, Michael Turner, Ezekiel Joseph, Whitley Ritter, Tenisha McKinnie, Robert Gibson, Edward Fields, to my awesome, amazing, cool, totally down to earth readers who stay on me every day about my next book and a ton of others I didn't name(you know who you are...), whether it was merely a hug, an encouraging word, a supportive shoulder, a random act of kindness that touched my heart, or simply being there whenever I needed you, thank you from the bottom of my heart! I really don't know what I'd do without you guys. Thank you so much for believing in me.

If I've forgotten anyone, my sincerest apologies. Just know that I love you. If you shoot me an email, I certainly won't forget to acknowledge you in my next book.

Peace and Blessings,

India

Chapter 1

Strolling into her large den, Bailey scrolled through her gold iPhone 6 until she found her slow jams playlists. Flipping the switch on her pink Beats by Dre pill, she maximized the volume and hit the play button. Immediately, *Late Nights, Early mornings* by Marsha Ambrosius began to filter through the speakers and into her soul.

Gonna be a late night, early morning when I get you home

Gonna give you good love, give you what you want and

Gonna do it all night long

Baby, let me do you all night long

Let me do it all night long

Bailey sang as she slowly moved her body provocatively with the music. Pausing long enough to light her Cake and Wild Cherry scented candles that she'd just received from Gifts from a Virgo, Bailey's makeshift dance studio was finally complete as she fell back into the grove of her music. She only had two days left to get the dance movements down before her next Body Shop Experts dance class next Tuesday.

Thanks to her overwhelming work schedule, she hadn't had any time to practice all week. While remembering and mimicking the moves from her instructor and letting Marsha pull her into the lyrics, her doorbell sounded. Glancing at her phone, she noted the time.

"Who in the hell is that at my door at this ungodly hour? It's almost midnight." Bailey rolled her hips all the way to her front door.

Once there, she peeped out the peephole to find her good friend and coworker of three years, Marcus Alexander, standing on the other side of the door with a box in his hand. Smiling, she shook her head as she unlocked and opened the door for her troubled looking friend.

Good heavens, if he was only my type. Full sexy lips, freshly pampered goatee, amaretto complexion, and muscles bulging from all over his toned body. Standing there looking like a tall mug of hot chocolate on a below freezing, winter morning. Too bad that only slim brothers with dreads or fros gets my pussy purring.

"Hello beautiful." His endearing smile further highlighted his handsome face.

"Hello yourself handsome. You're looking more annoyed than normal, come on in." Bailey shook her head in amusement at her friend.

Marcus was the coolest, most laid back, carefree guy she knew, but everyone thought he was mean by the way his face always seemed to be twisted up into a permanent frown.

"Thank you. Emily left me." Marcus blurted out as Bailey closed the door behind him.

"Oh no, Marcus I'm so sorry." Bailey was completely caught off guard, as she placed a hand over her heart. Marcus and Emily seemed to be a perfect couple; although secretly, she never cared for the woman.

"Don't be, I knew she stopped loving me a long time ago. And if I'm going to be honest, the feeling was mutual," he mumbled as he made his way toward the kitchen.

"Are you sure that there's no chance for you two to get back together? You guys have broken up and gotten back together many times," Bailey asked. She walked over to her fridge and grabbed a cold bottle of Evian water and wasted no time gulping it down.

"None. She's already on her way to get married to the dude she left me for."

"Damn. I'm really sorry Marcus. That's fucked up." She was utterly taken aback as the news continued to unfold.

"Forgot about it. It's nothing."

"All right fine, if you say so. It's forgotten. At least for now anyway. I do not feel like arguing with you tonight. So what's in the box?" Her eyes flickered with glee.

"Well, you know when I'm going through shit, I start cooking up shit."

"No, I know when you don't like to deal with your issues, you start cooking." Bailey countered, eyeing Marcus knowingly.

"Bailey, please spare me the psychobabble tonight, I don't need the lectures, I-I just need you to be there."

"Okay, I'll back off." Bailey threw her hands up in surrender.

"What did you cook for me?" Bailey asked, grinning as she peeked inside of the big brown packaging box.

"Parmesan encrusted chicken with broccoli, mushrooms, and asparagus pasta in Alfredo sauce, and homemade hand rolled breadsticks. I also have homemade orange sorbet and chocolate-covered strawberries for dessert," he said as he pulled the red lipped Rubbermaid containers from the box.

"I know you barely eat when we have deadlines at work and you know all this was going to go to the birds once it's cooled. So here you are." Marcus removed the last lid and sat the box aside.

"Marcus, I will never understand why you spend so much money on preparing these huge meals just to throw everything away. Why don't you donate the food to a shelter?" Bailey asked as she grabbed plates and glasses from her cabinets and placed them on the kitchen table.

"I tried, you have to go through too many procedures and fill out too much paperwork."

"Sounds like excuses to me, Marcus."

"Woman, you talk too much. Now hurry up and come over here and sit down so I can watch you stuff your face," he chuckled.

"Whatever asshole. Let me make us a salad and turn the radio off, then I'll join you."

"Okay to the salad, but leave the radio on."

"All right well here, you make the plates while I whip up this salad right quick."

"Cool."

Ten minutes later, Bailey and Marcus sat down to an irresistible dinner that was still piping hot and delicious.

"Oh my goodness, Marcus you should've definitely been a chef instead of a senior editor," Bailey moaned as she slid another forkful of chicken and pasta between her lips.

Marcus' dick instantly hardened as he watched Bailey slowly clean the small portion of food that she'd placed on her plate. Quickly, he shifted his eyes to his own plate before he did something he'd regret.

"So uh, how is your article on *The Wonders of Great Sex* coming along?" Marcus asked before sliding a fork full of broccoli into his mouth.

"Horribly, for some reason I can't focus."

"Well you better get to it. But knowing you, inspiration won't hit you until one in the morning when you should be getting your beauty rest."

"Hey, what can I say—when the pressure is on, I'm most effective. But enough about me, I'm worried about you. I know this breakup is taking a toll on you, whether you want to admit it or not."

"Bailey, don't be worried about me; once I get out her and get a few bad broads to comfort me, I'll be just fine."

"And by comfort you mean endless, meaningless sex?" She eyed him disapprovingly.

"Hell yeah!" Marcus laughed as he removed their dishes and began cleaning up.

"Marcus, you don't have to do that; why don't you go home and get some rest. Cleaning helps me sort out my thoughts."

"Bailey, you know I'm not about to leave your house like this. And since I just barged in on you, you go relax and let me take care of putting the food away and cleaning up."

"No I–"

"Damn it, Bailey you are one hardheaded ass women. Get the hell out of this kitchen before I carry your ass out."

"Geesh, I'll go. No need for empty threats," Bailey grinned and stuck her tongue out at him.

"If they're empty threat, why is your smart-mouthed ass making your way out of the kitchen?"

"I'm going to just ignore you, especially since I know that's just your broken heart talking. If you need me, I'll be in the den." Bailey rolled her eyes, waved him off, and was gone.

Chapter 2

As Marcus put the food away and began washing the dishes, his mind never strayed from the woman in the other room. When she opened the door in her favorite pair of black stretch pants and tonic top with her shoulder-length honey brown dreads pinned back from her face, he was ready to drop the box of food, pick Bailey up, push her against the door, and kiss her senseless. He had fallen for Bailey the day she first came to work for Unveil Health and Business Magazine three years ago.

There was just something about her truffle brown skin, big mysterious light brown eyes, left-dimpled cheek, and honey-colored dreads that spoke to the pure male in him; it was the kind, yet sassy, business mind that spoke to the rest of him. He loved the way her eyes lit up when she was excited about something, and the way she'd poke her bottom lip out when she was in the wrong and had to apologize. He longed for her relentlessly, craved to taste her thick thighs among other things, and he wanted to hold her when she was feeling blue, dry her tears when she cried.

Only problem was, he was already too deep into a three-year relationship to even try to pursue anything with her at the time. Bailey had no idea, but she was the cause of many fights in his and Emily's relationship, and one of the main reasons that his relationship ended. Since he couldn't have more, he settled for a friendship that turned out to be the best thing to happen—or so he thought. In actuality, their friendship turned out to be a double-edged sword.

On the one hand, Bailey had really been there for him, never overstepping the bounds of their friendship. Being that he'd never had a female friend in his thirty-two years of life, having a female around who he wasn't sleeping with was truly refreshing and somewhat strange, because he was a loner. On the other hand, he couldn't get enough of being around her, and that meant he would have to hear about the latest guy she was screwing, or try his best to comfort her through breakups.

After cleaning the kitchen to his liking, he grabbed the sorbet and strawberries, sat everything up on the red and gold serving tray, and went into the den. When Marcus darkened the entrance to the den and saw Bailey dancing erotically up against the wall to *Soulful Moaning* by Dale, he almost dropped the tray; he almost ran to her, threw her over his shoulder, and ran off to her bedroom like a caveman. Good thing Bailey turned around and spotted him when she did, or things would've happened the way he'd just imagined it.

"Oh, I'm sorry, just practicing for dance class, come on in." Bailey sauntered over to her speaker and switched the radio off.

"Uh-y-you could've kept practicing."

"No, that would've been rude—besides, you're my company. So let's sit, chill, and talk shit while we watch a movie like we always do."

"All right," he laughed to drown out his dirty thoughts as he walked over to the couch, while trying to hide the huge bulge in his jeans that was still expanding.

"So what are you in the mood to watch tonight?" Bailey fingered through her movie library, browsing for the perfect flick.

"You know I'm easy to please, I'll watch anything, but please just for tonight, spare me the chick flicks."

"Please Marcus, I am not trying to hear that bull crap, your ass was laughing more than me when we were watching *The Other Woman*."

"Whatever, I don't recall," he grinned.

"Yeah, I bet you don't. Anyway, we can either watch *Return of the Planet of the Apes* or *White House Down*. Or we could always pop in one of my favorite classics. *Love Jones, Love and Basketball or The Wood*."

"You know what, I'm feeling classic, throw in *The Wood*. I haven't seen that movie in years."

"The Wood it is." Bailey popped in the movie, grabbed the remotes, hit the lights, and finally made herself comfortable on her sectional next to her friend.

Marcus placed the tray across Bailey's thighs, grabbed his bowl of dessert, and watched one of his favorite movies with a woman whom he'd just realized meant the world and then some to him.

Chapter 3

"Marcus, this sorbet is amazing. I'm going to have to blackmail you into making this for me more often." Bailey licked the reminder of the dessert off her spoon.

"Bailey you don't have to blackmail me, all you have to do is ask me for whatever you want, and it's yours. And here, have the rest of mine, I'm done."

"No, I couldn't–"

"Bailey here, you know you want it." Giggling, Bailey took his bowl of sorbet, kissed Marcus on the cheek, and devoured it. "Ooowee, you could seduce somebody with all this deliciousness."

Tell me about it, you're doing one hell of a job at it right now. Marcus thought.

"So what are you getting into this weekend?" Bailey slid a spoonful of sorbet between her full lips.

"Nothing much, chilling, shooting some hoops with Anthony, then I'm going to try to drive up to the cider mill. It's already the middle of October and I haven't been yet. I've been dying for a dozen."

"Oooo, can I go with you, please? I've been wanting to go too."

"So you asking this time, huh? Last year you just came around the corner and hopped in my truck before I could even get out of the door good," he laughed.

"Well I'm asking you this time okay, geez—a girl's stalker side comes out of her for a minute and you never let me forget it," Bailey joked.

God, even her smile turns me on.

"You're crazy woman. What about you, any special plans?"

"Friday I do, it's Parker's birthday and she wants me to host a girl's night at my house, then she wants to go to a strip club. But Saturday and Sunday, I'm free as a bird. What day are you thinking about going to the cider mill?"

"Not sure yet. Maybe Sunday."

"Great. That's perfect. I can't wait."

"Yeah, I just bet you can't."

Bailey and Marcus fell into a comfortable silence as *The Wood* took them both back to some great memories. It was such a perfect moment until her phone rang. Bailey rolled her eyes in response to the name that popped up on her screen.

"Hello?"

"Hey beautiful, how was your day?" Cody asked.

"It would've been good had you not stood me up for the third damn time in a week."

"Bailey, I'm sorry, I just got so busy with work and taking care of business that I completely forgot."

"Save that bullshit for some chick that don't know you. I know better, Cody. I know you bailed out on me for another woman at the last minute. Just remember, you asked me out to talk. You're the one blowing up my phone, and who asked me to give your disrespectful ass another chance, but this is it–you get no more chances."

"Bailey, please don't be like that. I swear, I wasn't with another woman."

"Goodbye Cody."

"Wait, can I come over?"

"No. I'm busy."

"Why not?"

"I have company and he was just about to lick this whipped cream off my thigh, so if you don't mind, I have to go." Grinning, Bailey ended the call. Cody called back six times before he finally gave up.

"Son of bitch. Trifling, lowdown dirty bastard."

Here we go again. Why does she keep fucking with these weak ass dudes who keep breaking her heart? If only she could see me standing right in front of her...

"Trouble in paradise, my dear?"

"Marcus, don't start your shit. From where I'm sitting, neither you nor I can talk with our jacked up love lives."

"Hey, speak for yourself. I'm good."

"Says every man ever, after they've been dumped."

"Damn girl, you really know how to kick a brother when he's down."

"Hey, you started it," Bailey laughed.

"Seriously though Bailey, are you going to be all right? Do you want me to leave?"

Leaning her head back on the couch, she sighed heavily.

"No, please don't leave. I need my friend, a damn stiff ass drink, and a walk actually. What do you say?" Bailey stood and held out her hand.

She was trying her best to mask her hurt, but Marcus could see right through to her pain.

Great. One of the many advantages of being in love with your friend. Marcus thought.

"I say you've got yourself a deal, queen." Marcus joined her and took her hand in his.

"So what do you think, drink then walk or walk then drink?"Bailey asked on their way down the hall to the kitchen.

"How pissed off are you?" Marcus asked with a raised brow.

"I'm fucking steaming."

"Well, let's drink and walk."

"No, we can't do that."

"Why not, you think we're going to get pulled over?"he laughed.

"Shut up jerk. No, I don't think that. It's just that—"

"Bailey, pour yourself some wine in that big ass coffee cup you're always walking around with, get me couple of Coronas, and let's go. I'll be outside."

"All right, fine. But if we get into any trouble, I'm telling the police that you kidnapped me," she grinned.

"Yeah okay. Thanks for the idea, definitely going to remember that one for the future."

Chapter 4

Smiling, Bailey had no idea what she'd do without Marcus. Outside of her best friend Parker, Marcus was the only other real friend she had. She loved that she had a male and female best friend. While she absolutely adored her friendship with them both and wouldn't trade it for the world, Bailey especially loved her relationship with Marcus because with the exception of her father and older brother Benny, Marcus was the only other positive male influence she had. Grabbing their drinks, Bailey slipped on her North Face sweater and was out the door.

"What's this?" Marcus asked when Bailey handed him a large black water bottle.

"Your Coronas. I put them in there so it would be easier for you, and so you wouldn't be walking down the street with a beer sticking out of your pocket."

"Still worried about those cops, huh?" he gave a half smile.

"Hey, you never know. There's so many things that they could arrest us for that they just don't."

"Thank you for keeping my best interest at heart, baby... Scary ass."

"No problem. Jack ass."

"Touché." A sly grin crept across his handsome face.

Although unseasonably warm for this time of year and especially in Michigan, the weather was actually a little over sixty-five degrees and it was just after one in the morning.

"Wow, it feels so good out here," Bailey exhaled the night air.

"Yeah, it does. Wish this was our winter."

"Me too."

A few moments of comfortable silence passed between them as Bailey stopped to sip some of her wine and Marcus took a long swig of his Corona before resuming their stroll up the quiet block.

"So Marcus?"

"Here we go. Yes Bailey?"

"I know you don't want to talk about Emily, but I'm worried about you. And as your friend it's my duty to bug and probe you until I feel like you're okay."

"Bailey, I know you mean well and I appreciate it. I genuinely do, but please let this go."

"But you need–"

"Damn it Bailey, I mean it. And believe me, it's in your best interest to just drop this." Marcus dug hands into his pockets and tried his best to reign in his growing annoyance. He was becoming exceedingly uncomfortable.

"Oh really?"

"Yes. Let's just talk about something else. Have you made up your mind about going to the Halloween office party this year? You know, you don't have long to make a decision."

"Fuck the party Marcus, what's going to happen if I don't just drop it?" Bailey stopped, cocked her head to the side, and asked. She was beyond pissed.

"Trust me, you truly don't want to know."

"Oh yes I do. So again what—"

"I am going to kiss you. And I'm not talking about a soft peck or slight graze across your lips, but a thorough, heart pounding, knock you off your feet, make your clit start dancing to the sound of my voice kiss. You know, the kind of kisses you aren't used to. And while we're on the things that you aren't used to, you ever wonder why you keep ending up with the same kind of man in these dead end relationships? It's because you keep dealing with these men who don't know that they're supposed to be fucking men. And don't know how to put you in your place, but I am that man who knows exactly what to do with a woman like you. So when I say let something go, and that it's for your own good, I mean it Bailey."

"So what you're saying is that you've been judging me this entire time that we were supposed to have been friends? You're saying I'm weak, don't know any better, and that I'm a fuck up? Because that's exactly what it sounds like you're saying to me."

"No woman, I'm saying that you're spoiled and used to having your way and fixing people, which is cool to a certain extent, but I'm not one of your fans asking for advice, or your subjects under your camera lens that you can manipulate. So as my friend Bailey, please let this go. I'm not in denial, I just don't care to talk about Emily. Now let's finish our walk."

"You must be out of your ever loving mind if you think I'm going to spend another second in your presence after the way you just spoke to me. But before I go, let me just say that maybe had your ass been as observant in your own relationship instead of being all up in my shit judging me, your got damn fiancé wouldn't have left your know-it-all ass. You judgmental bastard!" Bailey screamed, then scuttled off toward her home.

"You want to know why she left me? Why Emily didn't want to spend another second with me? It was because of you. She left me because of you. How's that for intuitive huh?" Bailey paused midstride, then took off like a lightning bolt to her home.

Before she could even get halfway back up the street, Marcus ran up to her, grabbed her up into his arms, and pulled her between her neighbor's houses.

"Let go of me. You selfish, inconsiderate jackass. You intolerable jerk."

"Bailey I-I'm sorry. I shouldn't have cut into you like that. It's just that—"

"Marcus, there's no excuse to explain how you just got done talking to me. Now please let go of me."

"Do you accept my apology?"

"I don't know right now, give me some time."

Bailey knew that she would forgive him; she just wanted to make him squirm, and she needed a minute to compose herself after the bomb he'd just dropped on her. She was utterly thrown by his admissions, but there was no way in hell that she was about to deal with it tonight. She was still trying to hide her complete shock.

Holy hell, Parker was right. Marcus and Emily actually split because of me.

Chapter 5

"Did you hear that?"

"I didn't hear anything. Don't try to change the subject Marcus, let me go." Bailey tried to snatch her arm away from Marcus' vice- like grip, but it was no use.

"No, I'm serious Bailey. I thought I heard—Oh shit, I did hear moaning." His mouth curved into a smile.

"Marcus, please tell me that's not what it sounds like?" Her jaw dropped.

"Then I'd be lying because that's exactly what it sounds like. Want to go watch?" Marcus' eyes lit up with amusement and childlike glee.

"Hell no, I don't want to watch. What is wrong with you?" Bailey shot daggers at him.

"Come on Bailey, live a little." He nudged her.

"I live enough. Thank you." A muscle in her jaw twitched.

"Come on, just think of it as live porn." Marcus gave a half smile.

"Uh, hell no. We can't go to jail for watching porn, but we most definitely can by peeking in somebody's window to watch them while they're fucking."

"Geesh Bailey, you are such a wuss. Come on before they're done."

"No, I am so seri—"

Bailey couldn't get the rest of the word out of her mouth before Marcus scooped her up and tossed her over his shoulder, as if she was nothing more than a rag doll. He commenced to carrying her between the two houses and over to the opened window, where the loud moaning and grunting was coming from.

"Marcus, if you don't put me down, your dick and nut sack are going to be excruciatingly sore because I'm going to kick the shit out of you." Bailey was punching him in his back as hard as she could, but he didn't even flinch and continued to carry her as if he didn't feel a thing.

"Woman, stop making all of them empty threats before I really give you something to fret about."

"Empty threat my ass, I'm not playing with—"

Marcus raised his hand up and slapped Bailey on her backside so fast that she suddenly became utterly speechless.

What the hell? Did this man just slap me on my ass? And why did it feel so good. Since when have I been into being spanked? Focus Bailey. Now is so not the time to be horny. Or is it?

"Marcus, have you lost your freaking mind?"Bailey tried her best to sound mad, but she was sure that she was losing all credibility thanks to her tickled clit.

"No, not yet anyway. Just hold on for little bit. But if you don't stop tripping, I just might lose it and do all of the things I've been dying to do to you since the day we first met, so just loosen up and let's watch the show." Marcus sat her back down on her feet, being sure to hold her hand firmly in his grasp as he cautiously peeked into the cracked window and slapped her on her ass again.

A naughty grin spread across his sexy lips when he saw that Bailey had finally given into her curiosity and peeked inside as well. On the other side of the window was a woman on her knees, naked and handcuffed to a huge bed, grasping the headboard and moaning in pleasure. They also saw a man positioned behind her, grinding and pounding into the woman from behind. He gripped her waist and slapped her on the ass as he ground deep into her pussy, matching his grunts to her throaty screams and strangled moans.

Bailey summed up that she and Marcus had only been at the window peeping for literally just a few minutes, but she was already hot and bothered. She frantically scoured her brain for a way to ditch Marcus as soon as possible, so she could get back home to her vibrator and fuck herself silly.

"I've had enough, I'm leaving now," Bailey began to back away. Marcus held her hand tighter while adjusting his stance to accommodate his rapidly expanding erection while he fantasized about doing this very act with Bailey.

"Bailey, keep me company for just a few more minutes. Please?" He never took his eyes off the busy couple. Bailey shook her head and continued to back away, despite Marcus' firm hold. She proceeded to turn her head to make sure that none of her neighbors were watching when she saw a patrol car driving down the quiet dimly-lit street, riding the brakes.

"Oh shit, we're going to jail. I told your ass. I knew this was going to happen." Bailey frantically scanned the area for a place to hide.

"What?" Marcus asked, feigning concern. He wasn't paying any attention to Bailey because he thought she was pulling his leg.

When Bailey saw the brake lights of the patrol light up and the back of the police car begin backing up, she knew someone had called them and they had just been spotted.

"Marcus, let me go now." Bailey struggled to remove his hold on her when she whipped her head back around and spotted the front of the police car slowly come into view.

"Chill Bailey, they're almost done. I think," Marcus laughed to himself.

Shuddering from excitement and fear, Bailey was finally able to slip her hand from Marcus' grasp and took off toward the back of the two houses they were standing between, and had jumped the fence before Marcus could even place one foot in front of the other. When he turned around and watched the scene before him unfolding, Marcus swiftly followed suit and was fast on Bailey's heels. They had to jump three more fences before they came to a small opening, which led to the nature trail behind the local park, before they were able to slow down.

Chests heaving, Bailey and Marcus burst into laughter before spotting police lights in the distance and jogging into a cluster of towering trees that you could see right through in the daylight, but acted as the perfect mask of cover during smoky moonlit nights just like this one.

"Marcus, I wish I could kick your tall ass. First you're talking crazy to me, then you got me running from the cops. You're lucky I'm out of breath, jerk. I still can't believe we just did that. I'm running from the damn police, all because your horny ass wanted to look through a damn window to watch people fucking. You're sick," Bailey snickered while leaning against a tree inside their hideaway, waiting on her heartbeat to finally return to normal.

"Wait, I'm sorry, the live porno."

"Bailey calm down. You're so uptight. Loosen up, enjoy the moment with your scary ass. And while you're talking, I didn't hear you complaining at that window. Maybe that's because you were too busy rubbing your pussy through your pants. You didn't think I saw that shit, did you?"

"You know what Marcus, I don't know what the fuck your problem is or what has gotten into you tonight, but this is the second time in less than an hour that you have spoken to me like you don't have any damn sense. And I'm fucking tired of it. I know we talk shit to each other all the time, but you have gone overboard. Hell, I'd rather take my chance out there with the police than to be anywhere near you."

Annoyed, Bailey headed for the opening in the trees and was cautiously staggering out when Marcus seized her by the arm, spun her around, pinned her up against the tree, and kissed her so thoroughly that he could taste the subtle traces of sorbet that she had earlier on her lips and tongue. The kiss gave him such a rush that Marcus couldn't stop his lips and hands from subtly roaming all over her upper body. A shocked Bailey quickly fell under Marcus' spell as his kisses and slow caresses felt something like heaven on earth.

She had never looked at this man in any other way than a friend, so she was completely blown away at how swiftly her body yearned for him, how her nipples practically begged for him, and how much wetness pooled in her panties.

Who knew this man that I wasn't even the least bit interested in sexually, could make me feel like this? And is that his dick so thick and hard, going that far down my thigh? Mr. Marcus yes! My oh my, please let this man know how to use this thing. Yes, he feels so good. I just love the way he's holding me and caressing my body. Wait, what am I saying, this is wrong. So wrong. I think.

Marcus placed a gentle kiss to Bailey's lips once more before finally stepping out of her personal space. He stood back and just took her all in. Though he'd done this many times before, there was something about her leaning against the tree under the moonlight, the shocked expression on her face, her sex appeal, and her brazen personality that just brought out the pure male in him. His dick had somehow gotten harder just standing there watching her, exploring her, and mentally making love to her.

"Um Marcus, what was that about? What are we doing?" Confusion settled over her beautiful features.

"I-I'm not sure. But I do know that I'm about to do it again." Cupping her neck, he brought her closer still and sweetly claimed her sweet mouth once again.

Chapter 6

This time, not only did Marcus capture Bailey's lips in a bountiful earth-shattering kiss, he grabbed her up, carried her over to the thickest tree in the bunch, and repeated his blindsided seduction. Bailey was so far gone from all of the soul-shuddering pleasure that she didn't even notice that Marcus had slid her pants from her hips, let alone completely removed them, but she was very well aware of it the second he slid inside of her and her breath caught. Marcus hadn't even moved since he slipped inside of her, and Bailey was already soaking wet and bordering an orgasm.

Holy shit, is this really happening? Am I seriously about to let this happen? Well, if I wasn't, I shouldn't have let it go this far, right? Oh no, but he feels so good. Why the hell does he feel so good already? What am I going to do? I might as well enjoy it right? Right? No, wrong. He's my friend. Granted, my friend who currently has his dick inside of me. Fuck it. I'm going to let my hair down tonight and worry about the consequences tomorrow. I mean, after all, it can't be that bad right?

"Marcus—"

Just when Bailey was about to speak, Marcus quickly captured her delicate lips and began moving inside of her simultaneously. From the very first stroke of his extremely lengthy thickness, Bailey knew she was in big trouble. Her thighs hugged his broad waist, which he positioned her just right to receive every single inch of his glorious manhood. Though his dick stretched her drenched walls, it fit just right inside of her pussy, and was somehow touching every single spot in her pussy that made her scream, moan, and balance on the edge of an orgasm longer than she ever knew she could.

"Marcussssss!"

"Yes, beautiful?"

"I-ummmm—fuck yes, Yessssss. Harder Marcus."

"Are you sure, I'm worried about you being sore."

"I'm fucking positive. Fuck me harder Marcus, please."

She didn't have to tell him twice as his genuine, seductive, thrusting morphed into animalistic pounds of pure sweet delight.

"Yes. Right thereeeee. Marcus." Bailey screamed as an orgasm tore through her entire body so precise and so strong; she could've sworn that she was having an out-of-body experience.

Marcus was right behind her somewhere lost in orgasmic bliss.

"Got damn Bailey! Fuckkk! Your pussy is fucking awesome. Ughhhh," he grunted and moaned as he released so much seed deep inside of Bailey that he almost went weak in the knees.

"Shit!" He quickly moved his hands from Bailey's, grabbed onto the tree, and put his full weight against it.

A few minutes later, he regained his balance and carefully placed Bailey back onto her feet. This time when Marcus leaned in to kiss her again, Bailey turned her head away.

"Bailey baby, what's wrong?"

"I-I'm not—"

"Do you regret what just happened?" Marcus asked. He put just enough space in between him and the zipper as he buckled his pants.

"I-I have to get out of here."

Bailey rushed past Marcus while he was occupied and took off out of the park like a bat out of hell, and sprinted toward her home.

"Fuck!" Marcus elbowed the tree and took off after her.

By the time he jogged the few blocks back to Bailey's to make sure that she was okay and to talk to her about what just happened between them, she had turned off every single light and locked the front, back, and side door to her home. Heaving a frustrated sigh, Marcus took a seat on the steps of her porch and leaned against one of the brick columns of the entrance into her home.

I don't fucking get it. How could something so perfect, turn into such a disaster?

"Bailey, please stop this and open the door so we can talk. Bailey, I know you can hear me. Please talk to me baby."After a half an hour with no response, Marcus finally stood and got ready to leave.

"Bailey, I'm leaving now. Are you going to be okay?" Worry clouded his features.

He felt helpless and remorseful. He knew Bailey wasn't ready for this, but he just couldn't contain himself when the moment he'd been waiting to occur for such a long time finally presented itself; but the aftermath was now becoming more than he could bear, because he took advantage of her vulnerability. He knew Bailey like the back of his hand, so he knew that though she was pissed and loved to talk tough, she wasn't over Cody. When she turned the porch light off and quickly back on, he nodded.

"Well, I guess I can't argue with progress, huh?" he laughed. The light went off and on again.

"Are you going to call or let me come over tomorrow so we can clear the air?" This time, the light stayed on.

"All right Bailey, I'll let you be for now but just know, I'm only going to take this silent treatment for so long. You're going to have to talk to me sooner or later. Goodnight Bailey."

The light went off a final time. Shaking his head, Marcus made his way down the walkway and headed home.

Chapter 7

Bailey peeked around the corner of her lilac and black living room drapes and sighed heavily when Marcus finally disappeared from sight. Her mind was reeling with what had just happened between them as she sat in the dark, twiddling her thumbs. She couldn't believe she'd crossed that line with her friend. She now viewed Marcus in an entirely new light, a spotlight on a big stage with nothing but baby oil glistening down his torso to be exact.

No man has ever been so thoroughly attentive with me and felt so damn amazing. And his kisses were addictively pleasurable. So pleasurable in fact that my pussy lips are still puckering up for another round of body kisses.

Bailey shivered at the connection that she felt when Marcus repeatedly gazed into her eyes as their bodies made some of the most defining and alluring music she'd ever heard.

Oh no, what in the hell did we just do? And what was all that talk about Emily leaving because of me? Please tell me I'm dreaming. Well, maybe you would've found out if you had let his ass into the damn house smartass. She scolded herself. Marcus seemed to have her questioning herself a lot tonight.

"Ughh fuck."

Bailey fell back into her couch, slapped one of the pillows over her face, and screamed until she couldn't scream anymore. Once she was all screamed out, Bailey poured herself a second, though very generous amount of wine into her glass and headed upstairs to prepare herself a steaming hot bath. Twenty minutes later, Bailey was sinking her feet and her emotionally drained body into a brown sugar-scented bubble bath inside of her garden style bathtub. Bailey exhaled when she finally sat down in the tub, and the suds and warmth instantly began massaging her tired muscles.

"Wow, what a day; or a night rather. I don't believe I just let Marcus screw me outside in a damn park after playing peeping tom with him. And why, on top of all this disbelief, am I so horny and want Marcus to pound his dick in my pussy again? I really screwed up. There is no going back after what happened tonight. Shit, we work together; how in the world am I going to look him in the face after this? Damn it. And I know better than to be fucking my friends, especially when we work together and don't use protection. Jesus please be a fence, because I have apparently lost my damn mind."

Flustered and annoyed, Bailey placed her head in her hands and wondered what had gotten into her to make her behave the way she just did.

Fuck. I am so embarrassed. Why the fuck did I let this happen? And what am I going to do when I have to face him in the morning? This is just too much to deal with right now. Wish I hadn't turned him away though now, because I am horny as hell. I wonder if I call Marcus back will he come rub my booty and dick me down again. Damn he did everything right. Hit every spot.

Bailey reminisced while squeezing her thighs together. Eyeing her phone, she wanted to grab it and tell Marcus to get his big dick ass back over to her house now, but she just couldn't bring herself to do it.

"Nooooooo! No. Absolutely not. I am so much stronger than this—I think. I mean, I know I am. And I'm going to follow my first mind and stay as far away from Marcus as humanly possible."

Her next thought was to call her best friend Parker and give her the scoop, but she quickly decided against it. For reasons she didn't want to acknowledge, she wanted what had happened tonight to be the last thought running through her mind, and the image she wanted to picture before she closed her eyes tonight.

******

Marcus walked into his house and closed the front door behind him, in a daze. Dropping down on his black, white, and blue recliner in the corner of the living room, he causally surveyed the room as if he had just walked into his home for the first time. He had Bailey to thank for his odd behavior, because he was more than just a tad bit blown away by what had just transpired between them. Unzipping his pants so his throbbing penis could get some minor relief, he welcomed the flashbacks while at the same time trying to suppress them.

Never in this lifetime would he have bet money that his dreams of sliding inside of Bailey would've come true. With him secretly pining away for her since he first laid eyes on her, it was definitely a memory Marcus wasn't letting go of anytime soon. Leaning his head back, he closed his eyes and welcomed Bailey's moans and the way she moved, how she spread her legs and slid her pussy lip up and down his shaft. Marcus' manhood was so hard; he swore that if he'd even touched himself, come would explode all over him.

Balling his fists and placing them on either side of him, he tried to clear his mind and think of any and everything but Bailey. Very slowly, his body began conforming. With his dick waving half mast, Marcus stood, turned on the lights, and slowly trudged to his room. With the urge to stroke himself coming on strong, and since he was headed for the shower anyway, Marcus stripped and began stroking his cock. Moving over toward his king sized bed, he sat on the edge. All of the motivation he needed was present with images of a naked Bailey dancing around in his head, and it didn't take long at all for him to stroke his way to a huge, body shivering nut that completely drained him.

"Fuckkk!" Marcus slammed his eyes shut as he came in waves of deep, satisfying pleasure.

God damn that felt fucking amazing. I have got to get inside of Bailey again. Her pussy was just too good and her body...man, I just want to kiss, suck, and lick all over her, until she begs me to stop.

Walking into the bathroom off the left corner of his bedroom, Marcus grabbed a washcloth, cleaned himself up, and jumped his tired, thoroughly satisfied body into the shower.

I don't know how the hell I'm supposed to just go back to acting like myself around her. Now that I finally got a taste of her that I've been wanting so bad, I know I'm not going to be able to be around her and not want to kiss her or slide my dick in her. Our friendship is officially over, because I no longer have any desire to be her friend any fucking more. Not after tonight. And I'm going to tell her stubborn ass that shit tomorrow just as soon as I get her ass alone. She should have never responded to me like that.

Marcus reminisced of the way Bailey's body welcomed him as he continued to wash his himself.

And who the fuck walks around with a soaking wet pussy like that?

Just that thought alone got his dick hard again and before he knew it, he was almost aggressively stroking his manhood to the finish line.

"Ahhh shit." Marcus clenched his jaws and slammed his eyes shut the same exact time his thick, creamy nut shot all over the shower stall.

"This shit is crazy. I've never had this little self-control. Bailey don't know it yet but her ass is mine. Now all I got to do is make her see that, while making sure Cody's punk ass don't bring himself back around no more."

Bailey was the woman he really wanted, and now that he'd gotten lucky he wasn't about to let her go without trying to be the one to win her heart this time around.

Chapter 8

When her alarm clock went off two hours after she actually got into bed at five thirty in the morning, Bailey didn't hit the snooze button and mumble five more minutes like she usually did, because she never went to sleep. All she did was tossed and turned as images of her and Marcus just a few hours ago haunted her every time she closed her eyes. She was still in shock and couldn't believe that they had went there.

Bailey pulled her super plush comforter back and hopped down from her bed, carefully skimming her thoughts back to the beginning of their friendship all the way until now for signs of sexual attractions on either of their ends, but found none.

"Maybe it was just a fluke and I'm worrying for nothing. Maybe Marcus just wanted something to do to take his mind off Emily. Yes, that's got to be it. Marcus is still tripping over Emily and just turned to me sexually so he wouldn't have to think about the issue at hand. Which is understandable, but I don't like being used and he knows that. But good heavens, he felt wonderful. It was toe curling, bedspread fisting ecstasy. Who knew sex could feel twenty times better than it normally was?"

Frowning, Bailey skimmed her closet for something to wear to work when her annoyance at the entire situation with him became very apparent.

I wish I had been smart enough to ignore his misguided advances. Instead, I just listened to the throbbing between my thighs and spread my excited legs wide open. Shit. I don't believe I feel for his shit.

She didn't know if she was more annoyed with the fact that Marcus used her, or the way her body was shamelessly begging for his touch right at that moment.

Pulling a burgundy two-piece skirt set and white blouse from her closet, Bailey laid everything across her bed and hesitantly got ready for her day. Though she was excited about the ideas she had for their next issue and couldn't wait to get to the office to present them to her boss, she dreaded the walking past Marcus' office, and how in the world she was going to get through her day without running into a man that she'd shared pretty much everything with for eighty percent of the time since they'd become friends?

It's official, I'm increasing my porno stash and going to start masturbating somewhere between six to eight times a day. I'm sure that'll keep my hot ass out of trouble, right? I really hope so. Or else my hot ass is in big trouble.

Even as she tried to convince herself otherwise, she knew that trouble had just become her middle name, and if there was one thing she knew about Marcus, he loved to play with trouble. When Bailey made it to the office, she'd managed to avoid Marcus all morning and most of the afternoon, but just when she thought she was home free, she ran smack into none other than Marcus himself.

How come I didn't know how sexy he was until now? Good googaly moogaly, I just want to push him down on my desk, bounce on his dick, and ride him until we're coming all over the place.

Standing in front of her in black slacks, a starched button down shirt with his biceps practically bursting at the seams, and a red and black tie that she was imagining him tying her to his bed with, she was ready to strip naked right then and ride his face until the cops came and arrested them for indecent exposure.

All right, it's official, I'm going to have to stay away from this man.

For the first time since they'd become friends three years ago, this man turned her on like nobody's business; and if that wasn't bad enough, the way he was currently searching her eyes had her pussy soaking her lace thong.

Bailey May Johnson, if you don't go somewhere and sit your hot tail down! She scolded herself.

"So is this how you're going to act? I mean seriously, don't you think you're a little too old to be acting this petty?" Marcus asked her.

"Excuse me, are you calling me old and pe–"Marcus quickly caught her lips between his and kissed the attitude right out of her.

"Um, woman I love your sexy ass lips. So where were you running off to beautiful?"Marcus had completely captured her gaze and had her in an almost trance like state.

Hello? Earth to Bailey, quit daydreaming and tell this man exactly where he can go. And while you're at it slap him across the face for good measure for him kissing you without your permission.

Bailey cleared her throat and tried to speak, but no words came out.

"All right fine, don't answer. It's cool, cat probably got your tongue anyway. But just know that I don't do that silent treatment, I told you that. So either I make you talk or you find your voice quick. But I got to tell you, making you would be a fantasy come true."

****

"Girl, shut up. No y'all didn't. Stop lying?" Parker gulped as the shock of what Bailey had just told her quickly registered.

"Parker, I'm serious as shit and you know I am. Now wipe that stupid ass surprised expression off your face and help me with this mess," Bailey pouted.

"What the hell am I supposed to do?" Bailey huffed out of frustration.

Grinning like a mouse that finally was able to catch the cheese, Parker cut into her red velvet waffle and then took note of the warm autumn day and peaceful scenery outside of Kuzzo's Chicken and Waffles on Livernois in Detroit. Turning back to her plate, Parker purposely chewed her food slowly before finally responding.

"Bailey, I don't know what you want me to say or do. Besides the fact that y'all are some nasty ass freaks, I told your hardheaded ass when I first met Marcus that he was in love with your ass. I also told you that your ass was going to eventually lead to the demise of his relationship with that chick, because he is in love with you. So there is nothing I can do or say. I mean, well besides I told you so. But that wouldn't have made you feel any better about your situation. So I got nothing," Parker finished, trying to hide her amusement.

"Parker, I really don't see shit funny. And I would help you if you were in my shoes. Now you're good with problem solving and you're a damn counselor for Christ sakes. Help me find a solution," Bailey whined as she sipped her lemonade.

First off, you know I'm a sex therapist, asshole. Second, while I am good at solving problems, I see no problem here. I told your hardheaded ass that Marcus wanted your ass, but did you listen? Noooooo! You insisted that I was reading too much into nothing. Now that Emily is gone and you're between men, go for the shit. Throw your fears into the wind and hop on that ride again.

Hell, start a fling and see where it goes. You never know, he might be the one. What you do need to be worried about, though, is Jeremy finding out that his friend and the woman he's only wanted for years has been shall I say, is exploring new levels of their friendship. That man is going to be heartbroken and feel so betrayed by Marcus," Parker chuckled.

"Parker, Marcus and Jeremy aren't really friends. It's more like they just tolerate each other for Anthony. And this situation is so not funny."

"The hell it ain't," she laughed.

"Whatever, I'm not worried about Jeremy or Marcus. Ain't either one of them my man."

"Yeah, but both of them are sure 'nuff trying to be. You better get it together before I see you on The Jerry Springer show."

"Yeah right, girl bye. Not in this lifetime you won't."

"That's what you're saying now. Life is a funny thing. Talk to me in two—no talk to me in six months." Parker's laughter was contagious.

"Oh shut the hell up Cleo of the Physic Friend's Network. Who asked you anyway?"

"Uh, you did," Parker grinned.

"Well I take it back. So let's change the subject. What's going on with you? And hand me the hot sauce while you're yapping your gums."

"Nothing in my life is more interesting than your drama, and don't get all pissy with me because your love life is on the fritz. And speaking of fritz, what happened with Cody?"

"He stood me up again. Told him that's it. He gets no more chances."

"Whatever you say, Ms. Bad ass. Although, I just might believe you this time, especially with Marcus in the picture now, dicking you down," Parker winked suggestively.

"Parker, listen to me crazy—Marcus is not in the picture now, nor will he ever be. It was a one-time slip up on both our parts. It's never happening again. The only person that's going to be dicking me down is my battery-operated dildo boyfriend, Wesley."

"Ha! Listen skank, you can spew out all that *only one-time* mumbo jumbo all you want, but we both know it's only a matter of time before your hot ass is popping your thighs for him again."

"Parker I am completely appalled, where is your faith in me?"

"The same place your faith was in me when I was going back and forth with Austin's ass. Somewhere over on *Yeah Right Avenue* and *Trick, You Know You Lying Boulevard*," Parker laughed.

"I hate you Parker." Bailey tried to perfect a frown, but she couldn't deny the laughter that burst through instead.

"You love me."

"No, I can't stand your ass."

"Hey, if you want to live in denial, who am I to crush your dreams," she shrugged.

"You know, you're such a smart ass."

"Why thank you very much. That's the nicest thing you've ever said to me," Parker grinned.

"That's okay. Go ahead and laugh now. Soon I'll be able to wipe that cocky grin off your face when I burst your bubble."

"All right Bailey, since you're sooooooo sure of yourself that this thing with you and Marcus was a one-time only fling, how about you put your money where your big mouth is?"

"Fine, I have no problem with that."

"Good, I got fifty bucks that says y'all are going to screw each other's brains out again before the end of the week."

"Fine, and I got fifty that says it ain't gon' happen captain."

"Deal. And Bailey, I want my money. Don't come giving me no excuses."

"Well, as the winner Parker, I won't need an excuse sweetie. Remember that. "

Chapter 9

"Marcus, you straight man?"

"Yeah, I'm good. Why you asking?" Confusion temporarily deformed Marcus' centerfold features.

"Because Jeremy and I have been yelling for you to come help us carry the sectional out to the U-haul truck," his childhood friend and frat brother Anthony shot, mildly concerned after he and Anthony's friend Jeremy rushed back to Anthony's exercise room to make sure he was okay.

"Oh. Well I'm cool, got a little distracted wondering about my mom's health but I'm good now," Marcus lied.

Okay, so what I lied. But it wasn't a total lie. My mom was just diagnosed with high blood pressure and dementia. And I am worried about the hardheaded woman. But I may as well admit it, Bailey got my head fucked up. And I like it.

"All right, well come on. Let's hurry up with this couch and entertainment center right quick so that Jeremy can get out of here and go pick up Sammy from the airport." Anthony gestured toward the door as he turned around to leave.

A little over an hour later, all of Anthony's furniture was in the truck, and Jeremy was headed to his car.

"All right good people, I got to run. Samantha's plane touches down in half an hour. Tell Sammy I said stop by and see me," Anthony grinned.

"Anthony, don't make me fuck you up about my baby sister."

"What bro, you know I love Sammy," he laughed.

"Keep playing, hear?"

"Jeremy you know he's just screwing with you. Stop entertaining his ass," Marcus chuckled.

"Go get Sam man before she curse you from here to Georgia for being late."

"Right. Plus, Anthony don't want me to beat his ass."

"Hey, just hurry up and get to the airport instead of standing here doing all this yapping," Anthony shooed him away.

Jeremy eyed him challengingly before climbing into his car and speeding off down the street.

"Ant, why do you keep playing with him like that?" Marcus leaned against the front porch pillars chuckling.

"Man, Jeremy knows I'm just fucking with him. But let me ask you a question, what's really going on?"

"What?"

"I know how close you are to your mom and all that, but you just lied through your teeth back in the house. So what the hell is going on?" Anthony folded his arms and waited.

"Damn, is it that obvious?"

"Hell yeah. Now what's up?"

"It's Bailey." He ran a flustered hand down his face.

"What about her and how is her sexy ass anyway?"

"She's good. She's real good actually. I–"

"Marcus, you screwed Bailey?" The confession completely stunned him.

"Nah, we- I-Shit. Yeah, something like that," he groaned.

"What you mean something like that? Either you did or you didn't, Marcus. And from that lost, faraway look on your face, you did. You know when Jeremey hears about this, all hell is going to break loose, right? You know how bad he wanted Bailey to be his woman."

"Ant, I ain't worried about Jeremy, I'm worried about Bailey. She refuses to talk to me. She ignores me like she's upset about what happened between us. And it's driving me fucking nuts."

"She put it on you like that, huh?"

"Did she?!" He whistled and palmed his fists as the thrill of that night still surged through his veins. "That ain't the point though Anthony, you know how much she means to me."

"Well, why did you go there with her then?"

"I don't know."

"I specifically remember telling your ass not to be friends with her or any chick you wanted as bad as you wanted Bailey. But nooooooo, you go and—"

"Ant, save me the *I told you so* speech and try offering some helpful advice for once in your adult life."

"Listen don't get pissed at me because you slipped and fell into—"

"Ant seriously, I have to fix this shit. She's behaving as if she doesn't even want me in her life right now. I can't deal with that and the regret that was written all over her face."

"Well then you've got to go make her listen. You know what to do. Give it to her straight, lay your cards on the table, and tell her what's real. And speaking of your cards being on the table, what do you want from her? Are you trying to get the friendship back on track or are you trying to take it to the next level?"

"The next level. But I want the friendship too. You know how bad and how long I've wanted Bailey. I need her in my life."

"Well what are you still doing talking to me? Go make shit right. And try not to use your dick this time to get your point across," Anthony chuckled.

"You're a real jerk, but thanks for the advice though bro."Marcus stood, pushed back from the pillars, and strode to his car.

"Anytime brother. Anytime," Anthony whispered and gave a single wave with a twinge of jealousy.

Marcus was amped as he set his destination to Bailey's, but in the back of his mind, he couldn't help but to harbor some doubt and insecurity.

"How in the name of all that is holy am I going to get Bailey's stubborn, hotheaded, sensitive, overanalyzing ass to even let me into her home, let alone tell her that I'm in love with her and that I'm the only man she'll ever need?"

******

"Bailey, open up this damn door right now." Agitation was clear in his deep, demanding voice.

"No Marcus. Go away. Let's not do this right now. Please. I have a ton of work to do," Bailey spoke through her closed front door.

"If you open the damn door and hear me out, you can get back to your work."

"No. I'm not opening the door. I don't want to talk about what happened." She hit the door with her palm out of frustration.

"I don't want to talk either. I want–I just want to see you Bailey." The timbre of his commanding voice dropped several octaves.

"Marcus, I don't think that'll be a good idea." Bailey pushed off the door and walked away.

Before she could saunter into her kitchen to pour herself a shot of her favorite tequila, she heard a key turn in the lock of her door.

Shit, I knew sooner or later his ass was going to use that damn spare key.

"Seriously Marcus, just what don't you understand about a spare key being used in the event of an emergency?" Bailey asked when Marcus waltzed inside of her home and locked the door behind him.

"I'm sorry, but you gave me no other choice. And this is an emergency." He found the desire in her eyes and dared her to say otherwise.

"Really, how so?" She folded her arms and furrowed her brows.

"I had to see you."

"Marcus that—"

"Bailey be quiet and come here." He casually took a seat on the arm of the couch.

"Ha! Listen, I don't know who you think—"

"Bailey be quiet and come here, or else I'll carry you outside and bend you over your porch swing and have my way with you until the cops come knocking."

Bailey didn't know this side of Marcus and though she hated to admit it, she was suddenly flustered and more than a bit turned on. More important than that, something told her not to test this man because he meant every word. Doing as she was told, she joined him over by the couch. Standing next to him, Bailey waited for Marcus to speak while trying not to inhale the addictive scent of his Sean John cologne.

Good Lord, I have asked this man a million times not to wear this damn cologne around me. It just does something to me. And now that he's had some of my honey, it really does something to me. He's got Ms. Kitty misbehaving as we speak. Kitty I promise, if you don't get your act together, I promise I'm going to become celibate, she silently spoke to her anxiously excited womanhood.

After standing next to Marcus with no word exchange, Bailey moved her purse and went to sit down when Marcus gently cupped her arm and pulled her around in between his legs.

"Bailey I–I want to kiss you and make love to you until the sun comes up and bring you breakfast in bed an–"

"Uh hold that thought, I hear my phone ringing." Bailey backed out of their heated exchange and rushed to her phone.

"You have got to be kidding me?"

"Really Bailey, while I'm all in my damn feelings?" Marcus yelled.

"I'm sorry but I've been waiting on–oh this it's just Cody." Bailey padded back over to Marcus solemnly.

"What Cody?"

"Hey beautiful. How are you?"

"What do you want Cody?"

"Damn, I can't call and check on you?"

"No, you can't. And now isn't a good time anyway."

"Okay fine Bailey. I just want to apologize for–"

"Save you apology Cody, it no longer bears any weight with–"

"Bailey, give me the phone," Marcus said softly, but he was seething on the inside.

Putting her index finger up, she signaled that she would be right with him and turned her back to him. She continued her conversation is a low tone so Marcus could hardly hear her. Annoyed that she took a phone call from her jerk of an ex while he was trying to confess his feelings to her, Marcus had had enough and stood to leave. He was almost to the door when he decided to back pedal and deal with this issue right then. Walking up to Bailey, he gently unhooked her fingers from the phone and placed it to his ear.

"Cody, you're going to have to call her back. She's busy." Marcus ended the call and tossed Bailey's cell on the couch.

"Marcus, what is your problem? Why did you just—"

Marcus captured her lips in a slow searing kiss before she could get another word out, and before she could shove him away, Marcus backed her up against the wall and intensified the impromptu lip locking session.

"Bailey your lips are so soft and you always smell so sweet. Would you mind if I had a taste?"

Marcus firmly placed his hands on the wall on either side of her mane and gazed down into her alluring warm eyes.

"Um, do you really think that that would be a—"

"Bailey, answer my question baby. Would you mind if I had a taste?"

Hot damn, I'm loving this other side of him. He's got my clit longing for a nice long lick.

"Y-yes, you can have a taste Marcus."

"Thank you." Marcus eased to his knees and slowly removed Bailey's yoga pants and thong and before she had a chance to exhale her next breath, Marcus propped one of Bailey's legs over his shoulder, slowly sliding his tongue and lips across her drenched ones.

Wow, yes. Shit. He's sucking the—I didn't even know I could be kissed there.

"Ohhhh Marcus I—"

Bailey leaned her head back against the wall while she gripped Marcus' head and shoulders and moved her clit in unison with his long thick tongue as he explored her wetness. Grinning to himself, Marcus slid his tongue between her engorged lips and took turns gently sucking and lapping at her slippery slick folds, throbbing clit, and exploring her entirely. When Bailey tightened her grasp around his neck, he shoved his face deeper into her honey, and sucked on her essence like her very nectar depended on his survival.

"Marcussss. Ahhhh, ummmmm," she mumbled in between nibbling on the center of her bottom lip.

"Yes. I can't hold back any longer. I'm going to come."

"Well come for me baby."

Tightening his grip on her smooth thick thighs, Marcus slowed his sensual assault then sped up and slowed again. He couldn't help but relish in all of the intense toe curling, spine tingling pleasure that he was purposely showering Bailey with. He wanted her to feel him from here on out, every single time he crossed her mind and her thighs. Marcus finally decided to have a little mercy on Bailey; he stopped tormenting and teasing her. Slipping Bailey's pussy into his warm mouth, he alternated between balancing her pleasure button on the tip on his tongue and lathering her delicate folds until he felt her body spasm and shake uncontrollably, then he felt her creamy goodness coating his taste buds.

"Shit. God damnnnnnnn. Yesss," Bailey continued to shake as Marcus tried to suck the soul from her body.

Bailey felt as if Marcus was trying to send a message as she felt him tattoo his initials all over her pussy with his tongue. While she received the message loud and clear, she wasn't so sure that she was willing to acknowledge his artwork, or his suggestion to turn their friendship into a relationship.

No. I won't do it. Okay, wait maybe I'll think about it. No. Yes. No. How am I supposed to think clearly with his tongue sliding in there?

Chapter 10

"Ugh, I have a horrible migraine now. Great. Just great."

This is such a messy, sensitive situation, but I have to find some kind of way to make that bullheaded man understand not only where I'm coming from, but why he and I would never work.

Glancing up from her view of Woodward Avenue in Detroit, she sat in BIGGBY coffee at one of the tables in front of the massive picture window. Bailey took another sip of her Grande caramel macchiato and bit into her gourmet cheese Danish, then began to search her huge purse for her small bottle of emergency painkillers. Once she found and fished out the aspirin, she swallowed them down with a few swigs of water, and went back to the soothing view of her hometown.

Whenever her heart was heavy and her mind was in turmoil, she would come to this exact coffee house after work, have her usual coffee, Danish, and water, and perch herself in front of a window alone while she tried to figure out a solution to whatever was bothering her. Today Bailey had been there for the last three hours since arriving after work, and was no closer to figuring out an answer to her problem than she was when she first arrived. Part of her wanted to throw caution into the wind and let come what may, but the other more sensible side of her didn't want anything to go any further than it already had between her and Marcus.

Nodding her head no, she let her head fall into her hands. She was so irritable and restless. She wished that she could go back in time and erase the night they first had sex in the park. Temporarily shifting her thoughts from Marcus to Parker, she had two days left to decide where she wanted to take Parker for her birthday this weekend. She only had one more day to set some concrete plans, or she would never hear the end of it. At first when Parker said she wanted to go to a strip club, Bailey was relieved and overjoyed because she didn't have to do any serious planning; but yesterday when Parker texted her letting her know that she no longer wanted to go with her original plans, and that she wanted Bailey to plan something for just the two of them to do, she immediately felt a headache coming on because Parker was quick to shoot down plans and make suggestions after the fact; it drove Bailey insane.

Fishing her phone from her purse, she began searching things to do when her cell jingled, alerting to a text. Opening it, her lips formed a small smile against her will when she saw that the message was from Marcus.

Hello honey, hope all is well. Was thinking I could come over tonight and we talk and watch movies like we always do. What do you say, are you up for a little company? I promise I'll be good.

Bailey wanted to ignore his message, but she enjoyed spending time with him and as much as she hated to admit it, she enjoyed the earth shattering, cloud nine-floating sex they'd had. Right away, images of their escapades began to make her weak in the knees.

Um um um, what did that man do to me? I literally can't wait to feel him slow stroking me again, and that tongue was fucking amazing.

Bailey squeezed her thighs together to try to keep her throbbing womanhood from silently signaling to him like the people of Gotham signaled for Batman. After searching for a response, Bailey finally replied to Marcus' text.

I don't know. Ask me later and don't try to bribe me with food either.

Bailey hit send and waited for any further response.

Are you really going to make me wait?

He replied to her text instantly, and they began to text back and forth.

I really am.

Why, would you do that?

Because it just feels right. LOL.

Well since you're doing whatever you want to do to me, can I do whatever I want to you, when I see you?

Uh, no you may not.

You should. I promise, you'll like it.

Don't make promises that you can't keep.

How about I come over and remind you that I can keep every single promise I make.

Cheeky bastard. I knew his nasty ass was going to go there; but more importantly, why does it turn me on? Bailey grinned.

Bye Marcus. I'll talk to you later.

Yes, you sure will. Talk, scream, moan, and cry out for me. I can't wait to hear you beg.

Whatever, I wish there was a middle finger emoji. I'd text it to you right now.

And I wish there was one of a woman sitting on a man's face.

Ugh, you make me so sick Marcus.

No you have me confused with your ex, I make you horny.

Do you always have to have the last word?

I'll let you have the last word, for a price. Are you ready to submit to me?

In your dreams, smartass. Enjoy the rest of your evening.

You do the same sexy.

******

The next morning, Marcus sat behind his desk restless, frustrated, and operating on two hours of sleep. He was at work as he tried relentlessly to focus on editing all of the articles that were scheduled to go into the next issue of Unveil Magazine, but for the life of him, he couldn't concentrate, because he couldn't stop thinking about Bailey. He was already well behind schedule and since he was working with a small window of time in which he had to get everything done, he didn't have time to go searching for her around the office, or bother her at lunch, or text her dirty messages throughout the day.

Because Bailey refused to acknowledge the attraction between them, she made sure to steer clear of him and his office all day long, but he did manage to sneak a peek at her round, plump backside when she walked by his office with one of their coworkers when she thought he wasn't looking. A sly grin slid across his lips as he reminisced of the earlier memory of Bailey in a fitted, gray, thigh-length skirt and cream and gray blouse..

Leaning back in his executive office chair, he closed his eyes and welcomed the nasty images that had been dancing around in his head all day. Instantly his already half-mast manhood had sprinted upward full throttle, as if he was about to puncture a big hole into the crotch of his pants.

This is unreal, I wish her stubborn ass would just give into how I make her feel and we focus on everything else later.

Righting himself from his relaxed position, Marcus gave himself a no-nonsense pep talk and got back to work. It took him a while to finally focus but once he'd found his groove, he felt like he could actually put a dent in his workload–and everything would've went according to plan, had he not raised his head when he heard someone call Bailey's name through his opened office door. Jayvon, the graphic designer who had called Bailey's name, had just called her over to give her a card. They shared a short exchange, a brief hug, and parted ways. On her way back to her desk, Marcus locked eyes with hers and for a moment in time, they were the only two in the room; then just as quickly as their short connection happened, Bailey blinked, turned her head in the opposite direction, and was gone.

Annoyed, he rose from his chair and closed his door. He didn't know how much longer he could take her completely ignoring him, while she had no problem speaking to every other male in this office. Groaning, he'd definitely planned to say something to her about it.

Maybe I just should've left well enough alone because for as amazing as the sex was between us, I'd give anything to have her look at me and smile without worry again.

******

Several hours later, Marcus was finally done with his workload and ready to head home for the evening. Despite still being consumed with thoughts of Bailey, he'd managed to get through all of the articles and take care of everything that needed his attention. After packing up all of his belongings and personal items that he took home every night, he turned off the radio and light and walked out into the late evening sun.

"Summer weather in the middle of September in Detroit, now this is what I call perfect fall weather," Marcus chuckled to himself as he strolled to his black Hummer H3 and took in the beautiful autumn day.

Once he got himself situated, Marcus contemplated what he wanted to do first—hit the gym for the next few hours, or head home to cook and relax.

"What to do?" he pondered. "What I want to do is eat Bailey for dinner and slide up in her for the rest of the night, then wake up the next morning and make her breakfast in bed. But the way she's been avoiding me, I know that'll never happen in this lifetime. "

Starting his truck, he pulled out his phone and texted Bailey to see what kind of mood she was in.

Hey beautiful, are you ready to stop running from me and face this undeniable attraction and give us a go?

Not expecting a response anytime soon, Marcus was surprised at an immediate response from her.

Ha-ha! Very funny. Not. What are you doing? You leave work yet? Did you still want to come over tonight? I really miss us, our friendship. Come over and let's watch a movie together. I'll be home by 9:30.

Torn between wanting to be the friend she missed and the man he wanted to be to her, Marcus wasn't sure how to respond, but once the weight of her words settled, he decided to just be honest.

Bailey, I miss chilling with you too but I have to be truthful, I like this new direction we're in. I want you. While our friendship is important to me, I want more. I want to be both your friend and your lover. I want to make you scream with laughter and moan from pleasure. I want to bring you yellow roses for friendship and red roses for love. My apologies in advance for my brutal honesty, but I won't lie about how I feel. Do you still want me to come over?

Surveying his surroundings, Marcus hoped that Bailey still wanted his company, but he would go ahead and give her space to figure out her feelings if that was what she wanted. He knew that this was all a real shock to her, and that no matter how much she said that she was through with Cody for good, she still had feelings for him. Marcus figured the Bailey wouldn't just come jump on the bandwagon and get romantically involved with her friend when everything went down between them, but he never would've expected her to fight them becoming an item so hard.

He was raising his phone back to his line of vision when it alerted him to a new text message; Marcus smiled inwardly when he read that Bailey told him that she still wanted him to come on over.

Don't order out tonight or cook anything. I'll bring dinner. See you shortly.

Marcus hit the send button and pulled his vehicle into reverse. When traffic was clear, he pulled out and drove toward the gym. While he decided on what he'd make Bailey for dinner later, he couldn't help but wonder why Bailey wanted him to still come over, knowing how he felt about her. He'd laid all of his cards on the table and pretty much told Bailey that he wanted to be with her, but she still had yet to share her thoughts on them being an item, and Marcus didn't know how he should feel about that.

As he neared the gym, he made a mental note to just see where Bailey's head was concerning them, and if she was even considering giving him a chance. Secretly, he'd hoped that he was at least getting to her because after the last few days together since they'd crossed that line, there was no way that he could go back to just being her friend.

If Bailey still wants to keep me in the friend zone after this, I'll just file this under wasn't meant to be and just move the hell on.

Chapter 11

"Oh, so now you want to answer the damn phone," Bailey laughed when she saw Parker's name light up on her display screen.

"Look chick, you're lucky I'm answering now. I've got all type of mess going on right now. But that is still no excuse for ignoring my bestie, so what's up love? What chapter of your love triangle are we on today?" Parker snickered.

"Oooooo, you're so rude. But just know that when you need me, I'm going to treat your little mean ass the same way."

"Yeah, yeah. Just spill it chick, I missed the soaps today."

"Whatever. Anyway, I seriously need some advice on what to do about Marcus," Bailey whined and pouted as she drove downtown to dance class.

"Bailey, what do you mean you need some serious advice? You know what to do."

"Parker no I don't, or else I wouldn't be asking."

"All right fine, I'll feed into your bull this time. If you want to stay friends with Marcus, you need to go ahead and tell him that before his feelings get any deeper. He is in love with you Bailey, and he has been since he first met you. I tried to tell you that but you didn't want to listen. If you want to be with him, then I say you sit on his dick and see where this goes. Hell, I think he's a keeper and should be chosen over Cody's disrespectful ass any day."

"But Parker I still—"

"You still want to be with him?"

"No, see your slick talking ass think you know everything. I don't still love him per se..."

"Bailey if you don't stop lying per se," Parker laughed.

"No seriously, I don't love Cody but I still care. I mean come on, you of all people know that you can't just turn your feelings off for someone you used to love and share your life with. No matter how bad you want to."

"Yeah, you're right," Parker agreed when her thoughts took her on a quick glimpse of her past when she was head over heels in love with Daniel, who broke her heart completely in two. "But Bailey, you need to step into your big girls panties, pull them up, and figure out what you're going to do. If you want to work things out with Cody then fine do that. If you like it, I love it. If you want to explore things with Marcus then do that, but you can't do both. And at bit of advice from experience, if you really want Marcus don't string him along, or else you'll regret it. You may be stressed now, but just imagine how much more stressed and maybe even depressed you'll feel if you see the man you want fall for another woman. I'm still trying to adjust to that. So all I'm saying is, one way or another, you better figure it out before someone else figures it out for you."

"Yeah I guess you're right. Guess I'll figure it all out in due time. Thanks for listening and for the advice, Parker. I have no idea what I'd do without you," Bailey said as she pulled into the dance studio parking lot. She immediately found an empty parking space by the door.

"Bailey, that's what friends are for and lucky for you, you never have to find out. Especially since no one else can deal with your ass."

"Whatever. I have to go. I'll talk to you later broad."

"Bye honeybun." Parker blew her a kiss over the phone while snickering as she ended the call.

******

Bailey was exhausted by the time she arrived to home. Pulling into her driveway and into her garage, she cut the engine and padded up the walkway to the door. She was unlocking the door when a pair of headlights caught her attention. When she saw that it was Marcus, a small grin slid across her lips.

"Hey there pretty lady, I'm right on time I see," Marcus chuckled as he exited his truck and went to open his trunk.

"Yes, that seems to be the case. I see you have something for me over there, do you need any help?" Bailey asked as she watched Marcus holding a handful of grocery bags and still reaching for more items.

"No I got everything." He pulled another three bags from his vehicle before closing it and heading toward the house.

He was also up the porch stairs when two of the bags gave way and all the contents spilled down the steps.

"I suppose you need a little help now huh?" Bailey's smug sarcasm was written all over her face. She didn't bother trying to hide her soft giggles.

"Uh no, I still don't need your help smart ass. Now move out of my way woman." Marcus purposely brushed past Bailey and ran his knuckles across the curvy cheeks of her behind. Shaking her head at Mr. Touchy Feely, she went outside any began to help pick up the groceries.

"I told you I didn't need no help, woman." Marcus walked out of the door, ran up to her, and smacked her on the thigh.

"Put your hands on me one more time and you're going to be sorry," Bailey grinned while shoving him away from her with her free arm.

"Oh yeah. And what are you going to do if I don't? You know I love a challenge."He met her eyes with a heated gaze that held her captive until she quickly severed contact.

"Do it again and see what happens." She tried to turn away before he could see her smile.

"That's a ton of tough talk for a little woman."

"Good thing I can back it up, then."

"Yes you can." Marcus was temporarily lost in a flashback from their night in the park.

Returning to the present when he heard a car wiz by, Marcus helped Bailey with the groceries. She took a handful in the house and when she returned to help with the rest, Marcus ran past her and smacked her so hard on her backside that she dropped the food and almost fell face first into the grass. Turning toward

Marcus with amusement in her eyes just as she caught herself, Bailey took off and ran after him. Since he was a few feet away, he was almost to the end of the block before she finally caught up to him and jumped on his back.

"I told you not to touch me again." Bailey wrapped her arms around his neck and began to squeeze while playfully punching him in the back and chest. Her joyous laughter was like music to his ears.

"Okay. All right, I quit." Marcus reached around and tickled Bailey's sides until she slid off him and back onto her feet.

"You play too much. Made me break my damn nail," Bailey feigned a pout, and they moved back toward the house.

"I apologize. I'll pay to get your nails done over." He gently wrapped an arm around her neck as they neared her house.

"I don't like you Marcus."

"Ah sure you do. You love—"

The loud screeching of tires skidding down the street that stopped in front of Bailey's home brought their conversation to an abrupt halt. As soon as she recognized the of driver the 2015 Mercedes-Benz C-Class, Bailey knew exactly who it was and no matter how many times she stood there wishing the ground would swallow her alive, she had no such luck.

Climbing out if his car, Cody strolled up to them with the cockiest smirk on his face. Towering over Bailey at 6'4 with chestnut skin and a mouth full of pearly whites, she almost forgot he was her ex. Standing next to Marcus' 6'1 physique, she temporarily felt as if though she was in the presence of two expertly chiseled gods, they were missing from an expensive museum collection.

"Bailey."

"Cody."

"Marcus."

"Cody."

The tension was so thick that you could see the very second that they both poked out their territorial chests to the heavens.

"Bailey baby, I'll give you a minute. If you need me, I'll be inside. And don't forget that we have to get over to Moaners before they close." Marcus winked as he slipped his thumb into the loop of her jeans and backed her up against his crotch before dropping his hand to his side and going into the house.

"What do you want Cody?"

"Ha! He's a real character."

"I didn't hear you, what was that?" Marcus cupped his hand to his ear and began to retrace his footsteps.

"I said-"

"Nothing. He didn't say anything Marcus. Please go inside and I'll be right in." Bailey quickly stepped in between them to curb any possible altercation. She firmly pressed her palm to his chest.

"Yeah, Marcus, I think you should go on inside now. Let us grownups talk."

"Cody bring your ass over here and—

"Marcus please. Please don't." Bailey silently begged him to just go walk it off.

Clenching his teeth together, his jaw began twitching as he slowly backed up. Turning around, he slammed his fist into his hand and strode inside. Bailey knew it had taken a lot for Marcus to just walk away like he had. She was going to have to apologize profusely for asking him to be the bigger man. Inwardly sighing with relief, Bailey said a quick prayer of thanks before finally turning all the way around to meet Cody's intense stare. He had a smug smirk that she wanted to smack clean off his handsome face.

"Cody, why are you here and why would you come by my house unannounced? You know I don't entertain this kind of foolishness. What is your problem?" She shifted her weight to one side, slid her hands on her hips, and tapped her foot impatiently.

"God Bailey, you smell so good. Can I have a hug?" He reached for her arm and pulled her close.

"Cody you can't be serious. Did you hear a word I just said?" Anger flashed across her face.

"Bailey, come here and give me a hug. I really miss you." Cody pushed her hair out of her face and smiled warmly as he gently tucked it behind her ear. Her heart felt as though it was literally melting, but she reminded herself that she had to be strong.

"Bye Cody. And don't ever show up to my home unannounced again, or I promise you won't like what you see." Bailey turned on her heels and moved toward her house.

"All right, okay Bailey I'm sorry. I was wrong to just show up like this. It'll never happen again. I just wanted to see you. I wanted to apologize in person for standing you up."

"Fine. Apology accepted. Now goodbye."

"Wait, I-Are you- How've you been?"

"Good," she sighed.

"So you're dating your so-called friend now? And please don't lie to me."

"Cody, I don't see how that's any of your business. And you have got a lot of nerve telling me not to lie to you when you lied to me the entire time we were together."

"I'll take that as a yes. I knew something was going on between you and him. Were you spreading your legs for him while we were together?"

"Cody, you're out of line the way you talking to me. But I'm going to answer your ridiculous question just to make you feel stupid. I never opened my thighs up to Marcus or any man while we were together. Unlike you, I had no problem staying faithful to you. You did. I was loyal to a fault. So how dare you even fix your mouth to say something like that to me?"she frowned. Her words were laced with venom. Immediately, Cody turned and glanced down the quiet street as if whatever was going on down there was more important than what was in front of him.

"Bailey I'm sorry. I'm so sorry I hurt you. I really didn't mean—"

"Cody please, you sound like a broken record. Let's not go there right now." She waved off his foolishness.

"So are you going to give me a hug or not?" Cody cast a lazy glance her way once again, his eyes drifting down the length of her sexy curves.

"No, you can't have a hug. Now go home Cody and let's forget this ever happened," she exhaled as she ran a hand down her face.

"It's because of Marcus, isn't it? That's why you won't let me touch you right now, right?" Cody ran his hands along her arms before he turned his attention toward her home.

"Marcus doesn't have anything to do with—"

"I see how he looks at you, how he's always looked at you, and how you do the same thing with him. I'm too late. You're in love with him."

"Cody, you have no idea what you're talking about. Marcus and I are just friends and that's all we've ever been. But I don't owe you an explanation for anything going on in my life. That stopped the day you felt that I wasn't enough woman for you. So even if I was doing any damn thing with Marcus, that is my business. Now this conversation is over. Goodnight."

"Are you going to let me make it up to you for cancelling the other night?"

"No I'm not, and I never should've agreed to it in the first place. That was your very last chance to play with my heart. Bye Cody."

"Good night beautiful. I still love you and I always will."

Chapter 12

"So the happy couple is back together huh?" Marcus was leaning against the wall with his arms crossed over his chest. He'd been angrily pacing in the kitchen until he heard the front door close. He was pissed and he no longer cared if she knew it, but little did he know, he wasn't the only one.

"Really Marcus?" Bailey was seething. She was so upset that she began to tremble slightly.

"Really what? You're the one who—"

"No. Just stop right there. I'm not the one who did anything. You had no business trying to initiate a brawl. Are we adults or teens in high school, Marcus? Damn. And then you mention Moaners sex shop to be petty, really? Why would you purposely say that shit in front of him? Never mind, I know why–I just thought you'd have more respect for me." Marcus knew he was wrong, but he wasn't getting ready to admit it.

Marcus was so turned on by how pissed she was, and too preoccupied with undressing her with his eyes and half listening to Bailey, that he didn't register the end of her sentence. When it finally sunk in a minute later, he was furious.

"Wait Bailey, did you just say that you thought I'd have more respect for you?"

"Just forget it. Forget I ever said anything. It doesn't even matter anymore. I'm tired. Let yourself out whenever you're ready." Bailey wrapped her arms around herself tight and padded off toward her bedroom. *Oh no Bailey, it's not about to go down like that. I will not just forget about nothing.*

Before Bailey could take another step, Marcus grabbed her up in his arms and carried her back into the living room, and tossed her on the couch.

"Now please answer my question, did you really just say that?" Marcus wasn't even close to dropping this conversation.

"Yeah I did. Okay. I sure did. Damn. I feel like you of all people should've had more respect for me than what you showed out there." She was livid.

"Than what I showed? You're crazy." He pinched the bridge of his nose and chuckled. He stared at her in utter disbelief.

"No I'm not."

"Yes, you are. I can't even believe that you would even fix your lips to say that to me when I have shown you more respect in our friendship then he did in the entire time he dated you. You want to talk about respect? Cody cheated on you with every woman that walked by him the entire time he was with you, and he didn't even try to cover it up. And you still want to be with him. But you want to talk to me about respect?" Marcus shook his head and sat down beside Bailey.

"Marcus, I don't need your judgment. I was just saying that I expected more out of you because of who you are. I didn't expect you to stoop down to his level. But had I known that you were coming to throw stones at me from your glass house, I would've chosen my words more carefully," she spoke softly as she leaned her head back on the couch and closed her eyes.

Great. I feel like such an ass. Exhaling deeply, Marcus reached for Bailey's hand. She immediately snatched it away and sat on it. Marcus carefully leaned her over and pulled her hand from under her, and got ready to slip it in his pants. Quickly, she pulled away from him with laughter in her eyes before she finally cracked a small smile.

"I'm sorry Bailey. I shouldn't have went there."

"I can't stand you."

"I know Bailey. I love you too," Marcus grinned as he pulled her close.

"Nice try, but you've got to come with a better apology than that. We'll come back to that. What are you cooking me for dinner? And it better be something good if you want me to accept your sorry ass apology."

"It's a surprise. And trust me. It'll be finger licking good."

"Yeah, well I'll be the judge of that."

Bailey stood, stretched, and leaned over and grabbed up her phone off the coffee table in front of her. Soon as she did, Marcus smacked her plump, heart-shaped behind.

"I see you need another lesson in what happens when you put your hands on me? Keep on and I'm going to have to put you down." Bailey rolled her eyes and started toward her room.

"All of that tough talk is a big turn on. Don't say anything when I bend you over and spank that big juicy behind you're carrying around," he winked.

"You are so nasty."

"Thank you." Marcus stuck out his tongue and curled it suggestively in the air.

Bailey gave him the middle finger, then continued to her room. Marcus fell into a trance as he watched her hips sway back and forth, until her sexy body disappeared from his view. Shaking his head, he chuckled as he went into the kitchen to get dinner started.

Rolling up his sleeves as he darkened the doorway, he walked over to the sink to wash his hands when he realized that he wanted dessert first. The instant excitement caused him to rise full mast through his pants. Quickly, he adjusted himself as he took a few steps back and scurried out of the kitchen with desire fueling his steps.

With a naughty grin in place, Marcus followed the soft humming and suddenly erotic sound of running water as he neared the bathroom. Softly pushing the partially cracked open door, he strode into the steamy, cherry-scented space and began to quietly undress.

"Finally. It took you long enough. Was wondering when you were going to join me." Bailey said with her eyes ablaze with passion. She drew her lower lip between teeth and winked.

Grinning, with a heated gaze full of desire, Marcus joined Bailey under the stream from behind.

Wrapping his arms around her soapy waist, he nudged her behind the ear and placed soft kisses to her neck before pulling her back toward him, until Bailey's plump behind was caressing his dick.

"Well I'm here now baby and that's all that matters." He whispered while lightly grazing his finger across her thighs.

"Then pick me up and slide me down, I'm so horny I can't think straight. I've been dying to ride you all day long."

Slipping a hand from her hips down between her thighs, Marcus put two fingers into Bailey's warm wet heart.

"Lucky for you, you just made the height requirements to ride this ride."

******

Bailey's body ached from head to toe, but in a good way. Marcus had took his time last night and kissed, sucked, licked, and made slow, sweet, passionate and hard love to her body, mind, and soul all night long. They began in the shower before they pretty much christened her entire place. Resisting the uncontrollable urge not to skip to her car, Bailey beamed to the high heavens and as the sun tried to rival her the brightness of her smile.

Once Bailey was settled behind the wheel, she opened her phone, turned on her Bluetooth, and searched her call log for Parker's name. Excitedly, she waited for her friend to pick up so she could sing happy birthday to her. When she didn't answer, Bailey's elation waned as she had to settle for singing to her on her voicemail. When she ended the call, she scrolled back through her cell for her feel good playlist, which was a mixture of Jill Scott, Kindred: The Family Soul, Erykah Badu, and Kem, and drove to work with an amazing glow and radiant smile.

She felt so good that nothing was able to shake her good mood as she ignored the rude, careless drivers in the early morning traffic. On her way into the office parking structure while waiting for the traffic light to turn green, she noticed that the new cafe called The Orange Slice had finally opened its doors, and from the looks of things, the small cafe on the corner seemed to be quite busy. As she turned into the garage, she made a mental note to stop by on her lunch to check it out.

Pulling into the first available parking space next to the elevator bank, Bailey hopped out of her car, grabbed her belongings, and took the elevator up to her floor. Feeling like she'd just hit the jackpot, she strutted all the way to her office. Once inside, Bailey turned on her radio, put her purse and work bag down, and got right into her daily routine. While powering up her computer, Bailey reached across her desk for her notepad and pen when she noticed a small package and a baby pink card under her nameplate. Since she knew that her pictures that she'd taken for the company's upcoming issue were inside of the brown package on her desk, she pulled the card free instead.

Sniffing the card when she flipped it over, the faint scent of cherries and vanilla caught her attention. She grinned as she tore the envelope open to reveal a solid lavender *Thinking of You* card with a rose bush in the center of it. Opening the card, she smiled as the message simply read,

I'm always thinking of you. And it was signed, *Your Secret Admirer.*

Clutching the card to her chest and with a huge grin, Bailey wondered who the beautiful card was from. Glancing toward the door, she mentally scanned the office looking for who could've sent the note. Her first thought was that it had to be Marcus trying to be funny, but for some reason that just didn't feel like the type of thing he'd do without putting his name on it.

Yes. Much like he tried to do last night. She moaned as memories from last night's many lovemaking sessions caused her to slightly tumble backwards. Quickly, she reached out to her desk to steady herself. Pulling her thoughts away from last night, she wondered who else it could possibly be. She knew that as soon as Jeremy was hired in as the graphic designer, he was quite smitten with her and so were a few other guys that had made their feelings known among the office buzz, but no one had ever approached her.

"So they're pretty much ruled out as my secret admirer's right? Ugh, I don't have time for this right now. And I swear I'm going to ring Marcus' neck if he's behind this. Then I'm going to put him into this office, lock the door, and have my way with him."

With a picture perfect smile in place, Bailey placed the card up on the built-in shelving unit behind her desk and got herself ready to start her day. After her steaming cup of hot Joe, with one sugar and heavy cream, Bailey got down to work. At first, actually getting anything done proved to be a pretty difficult task with her thoughts zig-zagging between her secret admirer and Marcus, but by late morning she became a well-oiled machine as she handled everything that came her way. Even with her heavy workload, she was having a wonderful day.

"This must be heaven. I haven't felt this good in a long time. This day just couldn't get any better."

As soon as the words left her month, there was a knock at her door.

"Come in," she sang.

"Hello. I'm here with your lunch, Ms. Johnson."

"Oh I'm sorry, but I think that there has been some kind of mistake?" A puzzled Bailey eyed the food curiously as she made her way to the delivery guy ,who stopped in her doorway with two bags and a drink from the new restaurant she'd planned to visit within the next hour.

"No ma'am, there's been no mistake. You order was called in and paid for about twenty five minutes ago."

"Okay, can you tell me who placed the order?" Bailey held out her hands and accepted the delicious aroma of whatever was in the bag.

"No, I'm sorry but I can't. The person would not like for you to know their identity at this time. But I was instructed to give you this note. Have a great day ma'am." The delivery guy handed her a small card before he nodded and went about his day. Flipping the card over, Bailey read the note inscribed on the back.

Hello beautiful. Lunch is on me today! Enjoy. Your secret admirer.

Glancing up from the card, Bailey scanned the office for anyone looking her way, but found no one. Backing into her office, she closed the door behind her. Pushing her work aside, she sat her food down in front of her and just surveyed the unopened bag. She didn't know if she should be flattered or freaking out from whomever this person was. Bailey wanted so badly to silence her growling stomach with whatever it was that was filling her office with such an amazing aroma, but she refused to consume anything until she could figure out who this mystery person was.

In need of a break to focus her attention on anything else at the moment and to grab her something for lunch, Bailey left her office and headed toward the cafeteria as a million and one scenarios floated through her mind.

"Lord, please don't let me have a psycho on my hands. The last thing I need is a fatal attraction." She thought.

Chapter 13

Marcus could smell Bailey's soft, sweet scent before he even turned around. He was in the cafeteria eyeing the fruit station when suddenly her scent sent his body into a sexual hyper drive. He had to stand in front of the fruit stand after he chose his pieces because his dick had instantly sprang to life. Closing his eyes, Marcus thought of everything but sex and after a few minutes, Marcus Jr went back into hiding. When it was finally safe to turn around, he couldn't help the small grin that slid into place on his face. There was Bailey in a pair of copper brown and gold pants, like she just stepped off a fashion magazine. She was reaching for a turkey sandwich, and everything about her movements just to get the sandwich was sexual to him.

Damn it. What is it about this woman that I can't get enough of?

Marcus got ready to walk up to her and whisper something naughty into her ear when Jeremy severed his line of vision and ruined his plans.

"Marcus, how's it going my friend? Was just upstairs looking for you. Abby was taking orders for Chicken Shawarma's from Bucharest, but she's gone now. I ordered two just in case you wanted one."

Jeremy grabbed a big red Michigan apple, bit into it, and turned around just in time to see Bailey bend over to grab a homemade brownie from the dessert display.

"Jeremy, I appreciate you bro. Thanks man. I'll definitely take you up on your offer today. Other than some fruit and dessert, I was going to pass on lunch today."

"I hear you Marcus, but if you'll excuse me I see some dessert that I've been dying to get my hands on. Maybe today just might be my lucky day," he grinned as he continued to admire Bailey from behind.

"Ha! Jeremy I'm telling you, you just might as well get in line. You know Bailey's not going to go out with anyone she works with, not even for coffee, let alone on a date. You may as well give up bro. Throw in the towel, because that is just not happening."

Thank God.

"Marcus my man, you couldn't be more wrong. Well, at least when it comes to me anyway. I know you know her better than me because your friendship allows you to have that advantage, but I know women and I also know that woman is going to be mine."

Boy is this dude really delusional.

"The way she smiles at me, she's always concerned about me. I'm telling you, she's just shy. She doesn't know how to approach me because she's so used to men approaching her, and that's okay with me because I'm going to do just that. I'm finally going to approach her and ask her out on a date this weekend."Jeremy nodded and rubbed his chin assuredly.

"Okay, if you say so. Well good luck to you my friend. I see that you've got it all figured out. But remember when she turns you down cold, I just grabbed some tissue in bulk from Costco's to dry your eyes." Marcus chuckled.

"Hey, joke all you want but trust me, she wants me. I can feel it."

"Ha! All right then. Well good luck. I got to get back to work. I'll see you later."

"Hey Marcus, instead of running away you should've been standing here the entire time taking notes. I've told you many times that if I were you, there is no way that I would be in the friend zone with a woman like that. You should've gotten some of that a long time ago. Even if it had cost you your friendship. A woman like Bailey wants a slightly aggressive, take charge man. One that doesn't mind taking the lead. I know it's going to be a blow to the chest when we finally get together because I know you secretly want her, even though you say you don't and you passed on her for Emily's simple ass, who left you by the way. You're going to have to just suck it up and move on though. Cause let's face it, you're just not her type. I mean after all, that is why you're in the friend zone in the first place." Jeremy patted Marcus on the shoulder while pretending to dry his tears before cracking an evil smirk.

"Jeremy. I'd forgotten just how well you could tell a story. I'm telling you, you should've been an author. I have to get back to work, but you and your imagination have a good time over here. Clearly you two want to be alone." Shaking his head in disbelief, Marcus disappeared down the hall to the elevators.

****

Marcus felt oddly annoyed with Jeremy and slightly jealous of the fact that he and Jeremy wanted the same woman, who in Marcus' mind was already his. He was also irritated because unfortunately, Jeremy wasn't too far off his mark with his assumptions and points.

I am in the friend zone and I do want to be with Bailey. And hell, I hate to even see her talking to her sorry ass ex, so I know it's going to crush me when or if she chooses another man over me. And especially if it turns out to be Jeremy.

On his way back to his desk, he ran into Charity, a beautiful black and Asian woman with soul-stirring brown eyes.

"Hi handsome, how's it going today?" Charity's warm smile lit up the room.

"Hey Charity, I can't complain. How're you?"

"I'm doing good. I could be better but..." Charity purposely let her words trail off.

"Well, you're looking top notch to me.

"Um mm, so was there anything good down there?" Charity eyed him with sensual purpose.

"Depends on your definition of good." He returned her flirtatious undertones.

"Okay, well I guess I'll just have to check things out for myself. That's probably best. Well I better go. I'll see you around Marcus. You take care of yourself."

"You too Ms. Lady." As soon as he turned around, Bailey was standing in front of him.

"No wonder it takes you all damn day to edit. I forgot that you were a movie star around here," she pretended to yawn from boredom.

"I see that you're in a playful mood today, huh? Well, come on with the jokes then. It's really sad that you have to joke to hide your jealously." Marcus shrugged as he continued to his office.

"Excuse me? You wish. I'm not hardly jealous. If I wanted you I could have you." Bailey was dead on his heel as he entered his office.

"That's funny, but I never heard any of this tough talk when I had my tongue between your thighs. And you really was at a loss for words when I slid my d—"

"Hey, okay. All right, I get the picture. Just tell the entire office what we've been doing why don't you," Bailey chided as she rushed to his door and closed it.

"What's the matter, you don't want anyone to know that you like to be spread eagle in the park, picked up, and made love to up against the wall? And that you like to grind your sweet-tasting cat against my mouth when you're coming on my face and I'm drinking the very soul out of you?" Marcus closed his blinds on the spectacular view of the city before locking the door and pinning Bailey against the wall.

Marcus lowered his head to her and showered kisses down her neck and the tops of her full, perfectly-round breasts, and at the same time slid his hands around her waist.

"Somebody is mighty quiet now. And uh from the looks of those sexy nipples of yours and your accelerated heart rate, you not only agree with me but you want me bad. Am I right Bailey?"

Lost in the glorious feeling of tingling spanning her body, Bailey could barely remember her name, let alone any of his questions.

"Bailey?"

"Um?" she moaned softly

"Were you jealous?" Marcus asked while pulling down her pants. Before she could inhale, he'd slid a hand between her moist thighs.

"A little."

"Well baby, there is no need to be jealous because you're the only woman I want, okay?" Marcus slipped a couple of fingers deep inside of her while brushing the pad of his thumb ever so softly against her clit.

"O-okay."

"Good. Now, I have a little surprise for you, do you want it right now?"he asked while removing his hand from her silky soft wet lips.

"Yes, I want it right now." Bailey's voice became thick with need. She was lost somewhere between cloud eight and nine.

"You sure?" He lifted her chin with his index finger and gazed down into her wide eyes before pressing his eager lips to her slightly parted ones.

"Yesssss!" Her anxious moans quickly filling the small space between them.

"Good. That's exactly what I wanted to hear baby." Bailey was so far gone into a haze of ecstasy that she never felt Marcus scoop her up into his arms and carry her over to his desk, but she did feel the exact moment that he slid inside of her from behind and he gripped her waist.

"Ahhhh! Damn Bailey. I just love your pussy baby."

"I- oh-my goodness. I feel- you feel... Marcus, just fuck me please. I want you now, nice and hard." She bit the inside of her bottom lips as she felt his slow, tender strokes.

"Okay baby." Marcus groaned as he continued to slow grind in her and tease her until he was ready to pound harder and thrust faster.

"Baby, raise your leg up on the desk," he spoke softly against the shell of her ear. Immediately, Bailey shot her leg up and eased down on his upstroke.

"Fuck yes!" Marcus grunted when the new angle gave him deeper access and much better penetration. Pulling her hair with one hand and securing a firmer hold on her hips, he increased his speed as he pound and ground heavily into her.

"Fuck me," Bailey moaned, then slapped a hand over her mouth.

"That's right baby, muffle those screams, because if somebody comes knocking and managed to get the door open, they're going to be in for one hell of a show. Because I'm not stopping."

"Good, because I wasn't going to let you."

Chapter 14

Though the rest of the day flew by uneventful for Bailey, she couldn't concentrate on her work for the life of her. The only thing on her mind was the erotic interlude with Marcus.

God, that man really knows what to do to my body. Yes. It felt so good, but it was so wrong. There is no way we would make it in a relationship, but I do know one thing for sure. We have an awesome time trying. I just love Marcus so much that I'd choose our bond as friends over a possible disaster. I guess if I was going to be honest with myself, I may as well admit that I'm scared to enter another relationship, especially one with Marcus, and it fails. Plus we've been friends for such a nice block of time until I really don't see us being anything else. But then again, I didn't see myself screwing him yet, it's been happening so much that I'm starting to lose count. Not to mention how much I'm enjoying it and how fast and hard he makes me come. And how he does it back to back. I'll be damned; I have no freaking idea what the hell I feel. He has got me so confused.

Hey, maybe I should give him a chance just to see where in the world things go between us. It can't get any worse than it was when I was with Cody's lying, cheating behind. But the crazy thing is, I still love that no good jerk. Ugh, I need a glass of wine. Better yet, I need the whole damn bottle. Shoot, I can't wait to drink away my sorrows tonight. Speaking of tonight, I didn't know it was so late. I was supposed to be gone two hours ago.

After sending out a few emails and glancing over her desk calendar to make sure that she hadn't missed anything that she was supposed to do today, she organized her work area, tossed her food from her secret admirer, gathered up her belongings, and scuttled out of the office and straight home to get ready to hit the town with Parker for her birthday. Stopping by a convenience store to purchase some hair oil and a few other personal hygiene products, Bailey hustled to the checkout and then went straight home. As soon as she turned down her block, three minutes later her cell buzzed, alerting her to a call.

"Hello birthday girl. Happy Birthday! Where are you and are you enjoying every minute of being thirty-two years young?"

"Hey. Thank you love. No. I absolutely hate it and I hope this is not some sign as to how life in my thirties is going to be. I'm on my way to the mall to look for another damn dress for tonight." The annoyance in her voice was apparent.

"What? Why, what happened?"Bailey asked as she pulled into her driveway. She was so hurt that things weren't going the way her friend wanted them to on her birthday.

"I laid my dress on the bed and was looking for the shoes I was going to wear when I slipped on the pile of shoes while strawberry soda was in my hand. Spilled it all over my damn dress."

"Oh no, I'm so sorry Parker," Bailey nodded sadly.

"I'm so mad that I could punch a hole through a brick. I am so pissed at myself for being so careless, but

I was so thirsty. I should've just followed my first mind and grabbed a damn glass of water."

"Parker, lighten up on yourself honeybun. Everything's going to be okay. We'll have the whole rest of the day and weekend if you want it," Bailey tried to cheer Parker up.

"Yeah, well I'm not feeling like going out anywhere right now with the way I'm feeling," a defeated Parker huffed heavily.

"Nonsense, it's your day and I refuse to let you sulk."

"I figured you'd say that, which is why I'm out looking for a new dress. But I'm telling you Bailey, if I don't find anything I like, we're going to get ice cream first then pizza, and then go right back home." The defeat in her voice was breaking Bailey's heart.

"All right fine. But that's not going to happen. So cheer your sad ass up, go find you the perfect dress, and meet me at my house as planned. Got it?"

"Yeah, yeah, yeah. Well, I'm at Fair Lane now. I'll call you back shortly and let you know the verdict."

"All right. If you say so. But I'm telling you Parker, everything is going to be just fine."

******

Marcus couldn't run out of work and get over to The Orange Slice fast enough. Leaving his truck in the company parking structure, he walked across the street and stood in the long line to order his dinner. Jeremy had ruined his appetite, leaving him in a sour mood but with his appetite back and his not so pleasant mood long gone thanks to Bailey, he could finally grab him a bite to eat and relax for the rest of the night. Marcus had been there twice before and thoroughly enjoyed his entrees both times. Everything there was made with either oranges, orange flavoring, or served with a side of oranges.

He couldn't wait to try the next dish that captured his attention and made his stomach grumble. By the time he reached the order counter ten minutes later, his stomach was doing just that. Once he ordered the orange chicken dinner with extra chicken and an orange marmalade dinner roll, he took a seat in the waiting area while he contemplated adding dessert to his order. Marcus went to grab a copy of the Detroit Free Press from the lobby when the woman behind the counter came over to him with his carryout. On both of his visits, the same woman happened to take his order.

With wavy shoulder-length hair, a dimple in her chin, smoky gray bedroom eyes, and a small but curvy figure, she was certifiably a knock out. She would always smile and him and ask about his day. He half believed that she was trying to flirt without coming on too strong, but he wasn't positive because some woman just had a very friendly nature about them, but there was something different about today. Today, the way she locked eyes with him, though only for a fleeting moment, as she sashayed toward him had definitely told him that she was.

"Here you are handsome." She handed over his food.

"Hello there."

"I'm so happy that you're enjoying our food. Hopefully you're spreading the word about how delicious everything tastes..."

"Yes, I most certainly am."

"Good. Well I won't keep you any longer. But you have a great day and please come back to visit us soon."

"Most definitely." She smiled again and disappeared behind the counter. While strolling back to his car, he couldn't help but chuckle.

"Damn, she's sexy. And she was definitely flirting today. I wonder what her story is. Wait, forget her story, what the hell is her name? How do I keep forgetting to ask her that? Oh well, I guess it's best that I don't know, but I know that she can't keep eyeing like that, or else we're both going to be in trouble."

It's too bad I can't get Bailey to look at me like that. Speaking of Bailey, maybe I should just stop trying to pursue anything with her romantically and move on, because clearly she's got her mind made up.

Temporarily forgetting about his issues with Bailey, he focused on his constantly growling stomach. Unable to wait another second to feed the monster inside of him, Marcus climbed into his car and tore open the bag. Immediately, he became pissed because bedroom eyes had given him the wrong bag and he was starving. Because he was distracted by bedroom eyes, he never even paid attention to the fact that the bag was heavier than normal for one tray of food.

Upon further inspection of the bag, he realized that his food was there but so were two other dishes that he didn't ask for.

"Oh well, it's mine now," Marcus laughed as he grabbed the plastic fork from the bag and scooped a couple of helpings of his chicken and rice into his mouth. He reached for a napkin when he felt a card caught underneath it. Picking up the postcard, he read the company address, contact information, and the owner of the restaurant that was next to a bowl of oranges. Turning the card over on instinct, Marcus grinned at the message scribbled under a smaller version of The Orange slice logo.

Call me sometime handsome. And please enjoy the other two meals on me.

Beneath that was her cell, and the name Sabrina.

So you've the owner huh bedroom eyes, and you've got the hots for me.

Marcus tapped the card repeatedly against the steering wheel as a smirk appeared at the corner if his lips.

"All right Ms. Sabrina, I think I will give you a call. Yes, I think I will."

Chapter 15

Bailey had just zipped up her leopard print skirt and slipped her feet into her shoes when she heard her doorbell. Giggling, she rushed to the door and was ready to jump out and hug Parker when the sight of the delivery guy brought her to a screeching halt.

"Uh, hello. May I help you?" Bailey raised a skeptical brow.

"Yes. Are you Bailey Johnson?"

"Who wants to know?"

"Well I have a flower delivery for a Bailey Johnson that I need her to sign for but if you're not her, I—"

"Oh no, I'm her. I just wasn't expecting a delivery. I'm sorry, where do I sign?"

"Right here." The man held out his tablet with the delivery logo on it. Bailey signed and smiled excitedly as she handed him back the mini computer.

"Okay, thank you. I'll be right back with your delivery."

Stuffing his device into his back pocket, the man left and came back with two vases of flawless beautiful flowers,—one bouquet of red roses, and the other was a bouquet of yellow ones.

"Here you are ma'am, have a great day."

Before Bailey could say thank you, the man was gone. Stepping back into the house, Bailey closed the door behind her and sat both vases of flowers down on her coffee table. She went for the card in the red roses first.

Bailey, here is a bouquet of roses for you, just because I love the woman you are. Just think, if you were to give me a chance, I'd give you all of your heart's desires. And I don't just mean material things, I mean those priceless possessions that money just can't buy. Love Marcus. The other bouquet is for your bigheaded friend. Tell her I said Happy Birthday!

Bailey didn't know when her lips curled into a huge grin, but she was suddenly floating right past cloud nine.

Oh brother, I am going to ring that man's neck. Why did he have to go and do this? I'm not ready for this. Can this thing that really isn't a thing get more complicated than this?

Still grinning from ear to ear, Bailey was just about to lean down and smell the fresh, long-stemmed roses when her doorbell rang again. Rushing over to the door, Bailey peered through the peephole and jumped for joy as she opened it when she saw Parker standing on the other side.

"Yay! You're finally here. I am—wait, why are you frowning? What happened?"she asked as Parker brushed past her with a frown, and went and flopped down on the couch.

"You mean other than the fact that I didn't find not one dress I wanted in the whole damn mall? That's it, we're not going. So go ahead and break out the ice cream, pizza, and the Golden Girls," Parker whined as she fell back on the couch and covered her face with one of the throw pillows.

"Oh no, no no. We aren't going to do this. Get up and come on back to my room. I bought some dresses and a ton of other clothes last month with the tags still on them. So hop to it, because you're going to wear one of them. I did not get sexy to sit in the house and watch you sulk," Bailey concluded as she headed toward the back of her house.

Grabbing her cell on the way, she stopped in the hallway long enough to text Marcus a sweet, kinky *thank you* for her roses before continuing to her spare bedroom.

"Fine. Whatever," Parker mumbled sadly.

"Now Parker."

"I'm coming sheesh." Parker jumped up and headed toward the guest room, but she began to backtrack when she noticed the vases of roses from the corner of her eye.

"Didn't see these beauties when I came in. Um, what do we have here?" Carefully, she removed the card from the red roses and read it. Parker leaned down and inhaled the sweet scent of her yellow roses.

"Parker!" Bailey yelled.

"Cominggggg!" Parker sang. "And don't think I forgot Bailey. I want my fifty bucks. That skip in your step lets me know that you two have been screwing up a storm."

Two hours later, Parker dressed in a beige backless, wide-leg jumper with a plunging neckline, while Bailey wore black jeans and a brown sugar blouse as they walked out of the house.

"You look amazing. Now let's blow this joint and go have some fun." Bailey started her car and was down the street in the blink of an eye.

"Yes let's. But first we're going to talk about those roses on your coffee table."

"Dang, you're such a little nosy Nancy," Bailey laughed.

"Look that's not the point. And please tell Marcus that I said thank you so much for the flowers, because we both know that you'll see him again before I do," Parker playfully rolled her eyes at her best friend.

"Okay ma'am will do," she smiled.

"So when are you two going to make things official, Bailey?"

"Excuse me?"

"Oh, you have a hearing problem now?"

"Yes, I suddenly developed one when you started spouting that crap because I told you a million times that I wasn't going there with Marcus."

"True, but I thought you'd finally come to your senses. Give him a chance, Bailey."

"I can't do that. It doesn't feel right to become romantically involved with him."

"But it okay for him to screw your brains out huh?" Bailey peered at Parker from the corner of her eye.

"Oh baby, don't you give me that look. Anybody that knows you can tell that you're not only getting your toes curled on the regular, but you're getting them sucked clean, amongst other things."

"Parker, I have no idea what you're talking about." Bailey tried her best to hide her smile, but she was too late–Parker was onto her.

"Bailey, you better straighten up honey. You're going to mess around and let another woman come and snatch that man right from under you. And I'm going to be right there saying I told you so," she laughed. "And I'm serious about my money. I'll take all singles please."

"Seriously Parker, I get it, but not only is he my friend and I love our friendship, but I'm scared. I am so scared, or more like terrified, of loving him when I know that there is a big possibility that things will go wrong with him. Then I'll not only be walking around with another broken heart, but I'll have lost a very important part of me. I can't imagine my life without him anymore than I can imagine it without you. Outside of my family, you two are all I have. I'm just not ready to sacrifice that, no matter how much I love him."

"Bailey I understand. If anyone wants to finally see you happy, it's me. But I really think that you may be over-analyzing this one. I know you're scared, but if there's ever been a time to take a chance on love, I do believe that this would be the chance. No pressure, but take it from me–it's better to take a chance on love and be happy than to be unhappy because you have to watch the man you love be happy with someone else."

******

Once she was finally able to bury her thoughts away from anything that had to do with Marcus long enough to enjoy herself and celebrate with her friend like she should, Bailey had a ball. Since both she and Parker had worked up quite an appetite finding the perfect ensemble for Parker, they decided on dinner first at Brio Tuscan Grille in Troy, Michigan.

After an amazing dinner, the duo danced until they couldn't dance anymore at TV Lounge on Grand River. Now, almost three hours later, they found themselves at Northland skating rink, then Baker's Keyboard Lounge before finally welcoming a new day and calling it a night at Pampa's Bowling Alley on Van Dyke in Warren.

"Bailey I had the best freaking birthday ever, thanks to you. You are the best friend a girl could ever ask for. Thank you so much, buttercup." Parker's words slurred slightly and she reclined back in the passenger seat as Bailey drove them home.

"Anytime Parker. You're the best friend a girl could have as well." She shook her head and laughed as she wondered how much of last night was Parker even going to remember.

"I love you girl!" Parker screamed as she stuck her head and most of her upper body out of her window.

"Uh, I love you too loon, but why don't you trying to take a nap and I'll wake you up when I get you home," she snickered while carefully pulling Parker back inside of the car.

"You know, that's a good damn idea," Parker slurred as she fell back into her seat. "You're full of good ideas. You so smart. But you don't always act smart. Sometimes you do stupid things, like how you're letting Marcus get away. Stupidddddd," Parker sang, then begin laughing hysterically.

"Okay, thanks for the observation." *Wait until this chick wakes up from her drunken stupor. I got a few choice words for her ass.*

"Anytime Bailey."

A few minutes later, Parker was playing with her eyebrows and singing with the radio until she finally drifted off to sleep. Shaking her head in amusement at her friend, Bailey couldn't stop thinking about Parker calling her decision not to jump into a relationship with Marcus stupid.

I wonder if she really feels that way. My mom always said a drunk man tells no tales, but more importantly, am I being stupid? I don't think I'm being stupid, I'm being reasonable and slightly cautious. After all, it is my life and it's going to be my heart when it's all said and done. I don't know. Maybe Marcus is the one. Maybe he's that man. But I have no more room for mistakes when it comes to handling my heart. I have to be sure.

As if fate had stepped in with her sign, *Let It Burn* by Jasmine Sullivan came floating over the airwaves and right into her heart and soul.

"Ha! Nice try, but this song is played a million times a day. This song ain't hardly a sign. But like I said, nice try. Very nice touch."

Chapter 16

Marcus woke up feeling like a million bucks, but he had no idea why. He wondered if it was because he took Bailey on her desk yesterday, or because of the kinky message that she'd sent him as a thank you for her roses.

"I just can't get enough of that woman," he smirked as he rose from his bed and headed for the bathroom.

Marcus turned on the faucet and after brushing his teeth and washing his face, he threw on some old clothes and proceeded out of the side door and into the backyard. Moving around his truck, Marcus opened his garage door and went to his small workbench to grab his toolbox, two boxes of brakes, and his heavy-duty jack. Once he checked to make sure that he had everything he needed, he walked over to his Hummer, pulled up iHeart radio on his phone, and gathered himself to get ready to change his brakes. Soon as he sat his cell on top of the toolbox, *Let it Burn* by Jasmine Sullivan blared through the speakers.

"How ironic. I think I found the love of my life too. But her stubborn behind refuses to see it," he nodded in aggravation.

Who knew it was going to take this much to get the woman I've always wanted. But after today, I won't push her anymore. I'm going to leave the ball in her court and if she turns me down this time, I'll be crushed but I'll let go romantically, and just give her the friendship she wants. It going to be hard going back to the way things were though. Heaven knows I'm already addicted to the way she tastes and feels. And her scent, I can't forget her smell. Shit, it just does something to me and just like that, his manhood was looking for her as it stood at attention with perfect posture.

"No boy. Down. Not is really not a good time," he chuckled.

Stopping his task long enough to slam his eyes shut, he swiftly focused his thoughts on sports. Immediately, his excited friend disappeared.

"Yes! That was the last thing I needed to deal with right now. It's bad enough that I can't even be in the same room with Bailey without getting a hard-on."

After cursing himself for even crossing the line with Bailey, he focused his thoughts on the rest of his tasks that he'd planned today after he came back from the cider mill. He was determined to make himself relax at some point today, but he highly doubted that he would even afford himself the luxury since he had a tons of things to do around his home, and though he had everything edited and ready to go to the printer for their upcoming edition at work, he was still behind on a lot of other work tasks.

Four hours later, when he was done changing his brakes and washing his truck, he got straight into the shower and ready to go about his day. On his way out the door, Marcus slowed his speed long enough to make him a bowl of cereal and as he devoured it, he placed a call to Bailey to make sure that she was up and ready to go. They had a nice little drive ahead of them, so he wanted her to be ready but he had a feeling that just like always, she would keep him waiting forever for her to come out of the house.

******

Bailey woke up to her ringing cell phone buzzing right next to her right ear. Angrily, she snatched up the phone and tossed it across the room.

"No, no. No. It's too early to talk and why does it feel as if someone has been striking my head with a damn hammer? Call me back later." Bailey covered her face with her pillow and yelled into her king-sized mattress.

Hanging out until the wee hours of the morning had instantly taken its toll. She exhaled as a small smile flirted with the corners of her lips, but not even a minute later when the phone went off again, a smile was the furthest thing from her lips.

"No. I'm not ready to get out of bed. Please go away. I don't want to be an adult right now. I'm tired," she whined.

When it finally stopped ringing a second time. She was again relieved and tried to go back to sleep, but after lying in bed for about fifteen minutes, Bailey came to the conclusion that the land of dreams was long gone.

"Uhhh, why in the bloody hell didn't I turn that ringer off?" she screamed at herself as she snatched up her cell to see who had the nerve to bother her so early in the morning, then she tossed it right back down. "I'll see who it was after my shower."

When she gazed down at the time and realized that it wasn't morning but early afternoon, Bailey hopped up and ran to the bathroom.

"Damn it, I missed my hair and nail appointment. Aghhhh! I can't believe that. I slept the whole freaking morning away." Bailey stepped in the shower and stood under the warm water with her eyes closed. As soon as she did that, she saw Marcus' face first and then the rest of his body. Before she could blink, she was horny and wet.

This is madness. I just don't get it. How did I go from not being the least bit attracted to this man to finding him utterly irresistible? I want Marcus like nobody's business. Lord knows I truly do. And not just because of the absolutely awesome sex, but I value the friend in him more than anything.

Bailey finished showering and got dressed before finally going back to her phone to see who had been trying to reach her this morning.

"Speak of the devil," she laughed when she opened it and read the screen. There were two missed calls and a voicemail from Marcus. She quickly listened to it.

"Morning Bailey, guess you and Parker are nursing those hangovers from last night. Lol. Give me a call as soon as you get this message if you still want to go to the cider mill with me. I'll be leaving within the next two hours. If not, I'll bring you a dozen cinnamon donuts and a gallon of cider. All right, I have to go. Bye."

"Shit, Marcus sent this text almost two hours ago. That's it. Never again will I party that hard and go as many places as I did last night. I really had to have lost my damn mind," Bailey scolded herself as she massaged her temple with one hand and called Marcus with the other.

"Hey, did you leave yet?"

"No, got held up doing something with for my neighbor. I'm getting ready to head up to Blake's now. You still want to come with me?"

"Yes. You know I do," Bailey laughed.

"All right, I'll be there in ten. Please be ready to walk out of the door, Bailey. Don't have me waiting all day just for you to come out of the house."

"Whatever. It takes time to look this good."

"Well, look ugly today. I'll still want you."

Grinning in disbelief at his candidness, Bailey chucked her cell to the side and oiled and perfumed her body before she rushed to her closest. She threw on some jeans, a light sweater, and her favorite pair of black Sketchers. Dashing into the bathroom, she pinned up her dreads, put on some light make up and after inspecting her appearance, she was ready to go.

Just as she grabbed her phone, her doorbell rang. Suddenly, a broad smile settled on her face.

Just in the nick of time. Yes. Now Marcus can't say anything about me taking forever to get ready today. Tossing her purse over her shoulder, Bailey slid on her oversized sunglasses, went onto her kitchen for a peach, then walked out the door.

Chapter 17

Marcus couldn't help the huge grin the spread across his face when he pulled up to Bailey's house and looked on as she strode to his vehicle with her dark shades, looking every bit of hungover as he assumed she felt. Marcus was surprised that she still managed to come out of the house so well put together and just as beautiful to him as always, but then again Marcus concluded that nothing could take away from Bailey's natural beauty that not only shown on the outside, but shined just as brightly if not more on the inside.

"Don't you look mighty cheerful," Marcus' laughter filled his truck as he headed for the highway.

"Bite me Marcus," Bailey grinned right before she bit into her juicy peach.

She pulled the paper towel she'd wrapped it in from her lap and used it to dab at the corners of her mouth before leaning her head back on her seat and closing her eyes.

"So I take it you two had one hell of a night." Bailey smiled.

"If only you knew. And before I forget, Parker told me to tell you thank you very much for her flowers. She loved them."

"Good. I'm happy she did. Did you want to stop and get lunch on the way back?"

"How about we grab dinner somewhere tonight and just eat while we're there. You know Blake's always has tons to eat." She finished and bit into her peach again.

"Oh yeah, I forgot about that. You know it's been years since I've been to this particular mill. You know at Yates and Franklin, I just grab my donuts and go."

"Yeah, that's why I love Blake's, they have everything. It's like a mini carnival," she beamed like a kid reliving her childhood. "Well, you know how my morning was. How's your day been so far?" Bailey glanced over at him and asked.

Goodness gracious, how come I never knew that this man was so handsome? I mean really, my vision must've been temporarily impaired. I want him. Now.

"...and after I changed my breaks, I went next door to mow Ms. Nelson's lawn and take her trash to the curb."

"Sounds like you've definitely had quite a busy morning," she said, catching the end of his sentence just in time.

"I guess you could say that. So what time did you and Parker get home last night?"

"Honestly, I have no idea. When I finally did walk in the door, all I remember is lying across my bed. I don't even remember taking off my clothes."

"Haha! You're such an old lady," he playfully taunted.

"I'll be that then, because I could use another couple of days of sleep." Bailey finished off her peach, wrapped it up in the paper towel, and stuffed it into the plastic bag that Marcus kept in his vehicle for emergencies.

Once the laughter died down, they both welcomed the comfortable silence as they both traveled into their separate thoughts, until Marcus turned on the radio to keep any awkwardness at bay. It was such a peaceful moment, even as the unforgiving picture-perfect afternoon sunrays beat down on them as they drove up the Edsel Ford Freeway.

I've never thought about this, but Marcus and I have shared some really great times together. Even when he manages to tick me off, he's always does whatever it takes to keep me from staying upset with him. He's been such an amazing friend, but now he wants to be more and I'm not ready to lose this... these imperfectly perfect moments.

Casting a quick glance over to Bailey, Marcus held a small smile. He could almost see her mind going a mile a minute with things that he knew she had no business worrying about right now. He slid his hand into hers to soothe her. It was his way of telling her to let it all go for now, and to just enjoy the moment, but with the feelings she knew he had for her now, the innocent moment became too much for Bailey as she frantically searched her mind for something to talk about to cease the warm moment.

"I -uh haven't asked you in a while, but have you still heard anything from Emily yet?"

Removing his hand from hers, Marcus shook his head in annoyance. Purposely avoiding giving Bailey an answer, he turned up the radio and bobbed his head to the music.

"That's real mature. You're going to ignore me because I asked you a question. Fine. Be petty and childish."

"You know Bailey, you have got a lot of nerve calling me immature when you're the one that is behaving like a child right now. What is with you? Is the idea of you being in a relationship with me bothering you that much? Hell, just forget I even asked you if you're going to go through all of these damn changes. But don't imply that I'm being childish. You know damn well that I haven't talked to Emily."

"Marcus how was I supposed—"

"What part of *she left me and is not coming back* don't you understand?" Marcus was livid.

"How can you be so sure that she won't come back?

"Is that what all this is about, you're worried about Emily coming back?" His expression hardened with annoyance.

"Well the thought has crossed my mind more than a few times, along with a ton of other things about why we just wouldn't work."

"Well tell you what Bailey, let it go. Forget I even asked. Staying friends is the best suggestion that you could've ever made. Thank you for putting so much thought in it, but you don't have to worry about it ever again."

"Fine. But maybe you should go on to the cider mill without me. Just drop me off at Parker's." Vexed, she sat back and crossed her arms over her chest.

"Hey, whatever you want. Matter of fact, I'll do you one better and take you back home. I don't mind at all," Marcus hunched his shoulders as he came up on the next exit.

"But Marcus I—"

"No Bailey, trust me, we'll be there in no time." He produced a fake smile as he drove up the exit, turned around, and flew back down the freeway.

Neither one of them said another word to each other as he sped all the way back to Bailey's house. When he got there, Marcus came screeching to a stop in front of her driveway, leaned over her until he could grasp the door handle, and pushed the door open. Bailey was out of the truck and stomping up to her house. Before she could even get her keys out of her purse, Marcus sped off and took to the turn at the corner so hard and fast that Bailey wondered how the hadn't flipped over and crashed into another car.

"Oh well, I couldn't care less what that man does anymore. From now on, Marcus Alexander is just some guy I work with."

******

Though he'd never show it, Marcus was crushed. He just knew that Bailey was going to come around and finally give him a chance, not try to keep finding reasons why they wouldn't work. He hated himself for the way he'd just sped off so recklessly, and without making sure that Bailey had gotten into the house safely. He felt like shit, but he was tired of trying to prove himself and begging for a chance. Until today, he didn't know that he was so frustrated about the whole situation. He had never been so open with the way he felt to a woman before, and now he regretted ever doing do. Merging back onto the freeway, he started to go home or over to Anthony's house, but decided against it and instead decided to go to the cider mill himself.

"I'm just tired of her shit. A man can only take so much. And I hate the fact that she's just keep treating me like I'm some guy she just met yesterday. I regret opening my mouth and telling her anything. It was a big fucking mistake. But, from here on out, I'm going to make sure that I never ask her to give us a chance again. Hell, let her go back to Cody's lying ass. That's who she really wants anyway. She doesn't want a relationship with me, cool. And what in the hell was I thinking anyway, I'm free to do whatever the fuck I want. I don't have nobody to answer to and I'm going to keep it that way."

Blasting the radio to the max, he blocked out what just happened and enjoyed the ride to the cider mill by himself.

Chapter 18

Bailey stalked into her home and slammed the door behind her. She tried to stop the dam of tears that threatened to fall, but it was no use; before she knew it, hot angry tears were rolling down her cheeks.

"He wants to be an asshole then fineeeeeeeee!"she screamed. "He better not say shit else to me ever again. I don't know what I was even thinking about being with someone like him anyway. He gets this pissed off over a question? A got damn question? You do you then. Be an ass. I don't need you!"she yelled at the door.

Storming off to her room, she mumbled expletives as she undressed and crawled back into bed. Punching her pillows into the desired position, she huffed and shoved herself back onto the mountain of pillows.

"I don't need him. I don't want anything else from him. I don't want him in my life anymore period. From this point forward, we are no longer friends."

Rolling over on her side, she closed her eyes when she felt a ball of tears welling up in her again. Bailey wanted to continue to curse Marcus' name, but knew deep down that she was to blame because she wanted the argument to push him away, and that's exactly what she did.

I should've just told him. I'm so stupid. Why didn't I tell him? I feel horrible. But I didn't know that he was going to react so harshly. In all the years I've known him, he's never gotten that upset with me before, and he's been pissed at me plenty of times over the course of our friendship.

Sighing, she nervously bit her nails and propped her arms up across her face.

Maybe I should call him and apologize. Or maybe we're both better off if I just leave well enough alone. This way there is no confusion. He can go on with his life and I can go on with mine.

Between the migraine that had suddenly come from out of nowhere and the shock of the rift that Bailey had just shoved between her and Marcus, she tried her best to calm her mind and body long enough to drift off to sleep. It took lots of tossing and turning but forty-five minutes later, she was sound asleep. When Bailey awoke this time, she was met by star-speckled skies and a perfectly pristine low hanging moon adorning its center. Bailey smiled and held it as she stared lovingly into natural perfection until it finally donned on her just how late it was.

"It's dark outside already? That was quick. How long have I been sleep?" Puzzled, Bailey hopped up and reached for her cell. Pushing the power button on her device, she read the screen and frowned.

"It's ten to eleven. Wow. I really must've been tired. But once again I had a ton of things to do today and I have gotten absolutely nothing accomplished. Fuck."

Perched on the edge of her bed, she sat staring out of the window thinking about everything that happened that day, and immediately her shoulders slumped. She still couldn't believe that of everything they had been through, their time together had ended so harshly. Of all of the arguments and fussing over the years, neither she nor Marcus had ever been this enraged with each other.

Stretching, Bailey slid down from her bed, slipped her feet into her house shoes, and made her way to her kitchen as she rubbed her stomach. She was starving and felt as if she could die of thirst if she didn't get her hands on a glass of water right now.

Making her way straight to her refrigerator as soon as she stepped foot into the kitchen, Bailey removed the gallon of distilled water and a glass from the cabinet before sitting down at the kitchen table. She drank a full glass and poured herself a second glass, downing over half of that before she was finally satisfied. Browsing the three boxes of cereal on top of her refrigerator, Bailey grabbed a bowl and spoon and sat down to a big bowl of Fruit Loops. As she ate, she contemplated what she would make herself for dinner. When she remembered that she had made a late night run to the grocery store a few nights back, Bailey decided to make a small pan of spring rolls and a couple of egg foo young patties. After finishing her cereal, she sat out all of her ingredients that she would need on the kitchen counter.

Before getting started, Bailey went to check her mail to see if her coffee and phone case from Amazon had been delivered. Still in a sour mood, Bailey padded into the front room and stopped short when she saw a dozen donuts and a gallon of apple cider sitting on her coffee table. Looking around, she listened for any sign of Marcus moving around the house, but when several moments passed with complete silence, she walked over to the table. Upon closer inspection, she found her spare key that she'd given Marcus in the event of an emergency, and a note sitting on top of the small pile of mail next to the cider. Opening the note, she took a seat and began to read.

I know how bad you wanted your donuts and cider, so against my better judgment here you are. Take care of yourself Bailey.

Marcus

"No, no, no. Not like this, I was just pissed off, Marcus. Please don't do this to me. I'm sorry, I should've just told you that I was scared. Scared of loving you."

With tears in her eyes, Bailey ran to her phone and clicked on Marcus' name while she waited on the call to connect. After ringing five times, the phone went straight to his voicemail. Hanging up, she hit redial and waited again. This time and for her next several attempts after, Marcus sent her straight to voicemail.

Rushing upstairs, she dressed in a tank and jeans and headed for her door. Hopping in her car, she jerked herself in reverse and sped down the street and around the corner. Not even two minutes later, she was pulling into Marcus' home. From her car, she could see the minute Marcus got up from the lawn chair he was lounging in and walked inside of his home. Bailey had just climbed out of her car when Marcus closed the door and turned off the porch light. Furious, Bailey stormed up the stairs and rang the doorbell.

"Marcus, open the door please. We need to talk."

When there was no response from the other side of the door, Bailey began knocking relentlessly. When there was still no answer, Bailey went to the window and knocked again, but again Marcus refused to answer.

"Marcus? Can we talk please? Just give me five minutes please? I get it okay, I get it." Again, Marcus ignored her.

Feeling dejected, Bailey came back to the front door and rang the bell one last time. This time when she was met with no reply, her tears now fell freely as she ran back to her car. Feeling as though she'd just made a fool of herself, she drove away with tons of regret and her now broken heart weighing heavy in her hands.

******

Marcus woke up in bed the next morning feeling like a total heel. He felt an instant loss. Grinding his teeth, he massaged his chin as he stared into the abyss. Swinging his legs over the bed, Marcus took a deep breath and headed straight for the shower. As he stood under the shower and listened to the steady stream of rivulets of hot water pounding and sliding down his body, he wondered what Bailey was doing at that very moment. He wanted to call and stop by and check in on her, and bring her breakfast like he'd done many times before to see the smile on her face, but he refused to do any of that now because he was pissed.

"Why should I go over there? I refuse to go back and forth with her any longer. She wanted to push me away and she's succeeded. I'm done."

Stepping out of the shower, Marcus dressed and headed to work. When he got off the elevator, the first person he made eye contact with was Bailey. She looked so sexy in the fitted, mocha and chocolate-hued dress, until Marcus almost forgot that he was pissed at her. Their intense contact seemed to heat up the entire office, until Bailey quickly glanced away as she sashayed off to the office supply room. Angry for getting caught up in and mesmerized by her beauty, Marcus stormed into his office and closed the door behind him.

Right away, he threw himself into his work, working through breaks and lunch. By the time he looked up to check the time, it was a quarter to five. He was exhausted and practically panting for a cold beverage and something to eat. While packing up for the night, there was a knock at his door. After contemplating for a moment whether or not if he wanted to acknowledge the unwanted visitor, he decided what the hell; he was on his way out anyway, so if he didn't want to be bothered, he would politely blow them off on his way out of the office.

"Come in."

"Hey handsome. How are you?" His coworker Trina Lovely from marketing waltzed into his office, smiling from ear to ear.

"Hey, I'm good beautiful. What's going on?" Marcus asked as he continued cleaning up workspace.

"Oh nothing. A few of us are about to head over to Swizzle Sticks to have a few after work drinks, and we wanted to know if you wanted to come along." Trina cozied up to Marcus and asked sweetly.

Grinning immediately, Marcus put some space between them. He was positive that going anywhere with this woman wasn't a good idea, because she was having a hard time accepting the fact that he wasn't interested, but after work drinks did sound damn good to him—especially while he was still dealing with everything that had just happened with Bailey.

Trina had been trying to get Marcus in her clutches since his first day on the job, and though he'd politely refused every single time, she just kept right on coming in hopes of trying to wear him down like she'd done every other man in the office that she' wanted. So far, he was the only man she hadn't been able to shake. Marcus would've been happy to spend a little alone time with her because she was incredibly sexy with her creamy, sandy brown skin, onyx eyes, and thin but shapely frame, but she was too aggressive, too sneaky, and too money hungry for his taste, which in turn made her look very unattractive.

"You know, I think I will join you all for a bit," Marcus finally responded.

He was desperate for anything to take his mind off Bailey, and a couple of hours of drinks and laughs with a mostly great team of people would definitely do the trick. Marcus would rather have met up with Anthony or one of his other close childhood friends, but everyone was currently at work so he decided to take whatever distraction he could get.

"Great," Trina grinned, slowly moving into his personal space again. "Did you want to ride over with me?" she beamed.

"Thanks for the offer Trina, but I have a few things to do here before I head out."

"Oh well, I could wait for you to finish up if you'd like. It would be no problem at all."

"No Trina, you go ahead. I'll just see you all there in a few."

"All right, well if you insist." Marcus was relieved when she finally stopped trying to push the issue.

"See you shortly sexy," Trina winked and sashayed out of office, just as Bailey was strolling by blocking her path toward the exit.

"Bailey, hey honey. I was just looking for you," Trina plastered on her best false grin. Bailey glanced from her to Marcus, then into his office before replying,

"Really now. Well you know I've been in the same place all day; in my office."

"I must've just overlooked you then. But let's not dwell on the past, I just wanted to invite you out to have drinks with most of the office. We'll all heading over there now. I was just inviting Marcus and after a little persuasion, I finally got him to agree to join us," she turned to Marcus and winked.

"A little persuasion is all it took, huh?"

"Yup. I'm sure you know all of that since you two are such good friends and whatnot."

"Right. I know all about it. Anyway, thanks for the offer but I'm going to have to decline. I have a hot date tonight. You know how that this, trying to make sure you're perfect for that special someone." She cast a quick glance at Marcus, with a smirk tickling the corners of her lips before focusing her attention back to Trina.

"Yes, I know all about it. And let me just say, I am so happy for you. I mean, that you have a date. Well, let me slide on out of your way so you don't leave that special guy waiting. We'll, be sure to have a drink or two for you though. So don't worry about a thing. It'll be just as if you were right there with us. Right Marcus?" Trina slid up next to Marcus and slipped her hand into his.

"Yup. Absolutely". He locked Bailey into an intense stare before turning his attention back to Trina.

"Well, that's very kind of you Trina. And you too Marcus. Y'all have a good night now," Bailey laughed as she continued on out of the office to her car.

By the time she made it to the elevator and turned around, she rolled her eyes while placing her middle and index finger to her right temple. She gently massaged the area when she saw that Marcus' new friend had sauntered off, and she now had his undivided attention. As the doors closed, she held a small smile as she waved at him and mouthed the words, *have fun.*

Though he was annoyed, he wasn't about to let Bailey get the best of him or the last word so he mouthed back, *I will*, and winked just as the doors closed. Walking back into his office, he snickered to himself.

"If I'm going to be miserable, her ass is too."

Chapter 19

"Please tell me this is your idea of a bad joke and that you didn't really push that man away, Bailey?"Parker shook her head in disappointment. She dropped her head in her hand in frustration.

"Parker, I didn't push him away he—"

"He what Bailey? What did he do?"

"He—"

"Did absolutely nothing but try repeatedly to be with your stubborn ass." Parker slammed the palm of her hand on the patio table at Ocean Prime in Troy.

"Parker, are you going to let me finish? And whose damn side are you on?" She shot Parker a nasty frown of disapproval as she slouched back in her seat.

Exhaling, Parker leaned back in her seat and took in the stunning view around them as people went about their daily lives. Other than the two of them enjoying their lunch, there was no one else outside. Parker welcomed the much-needed peace and privacy as she tried to find the right words to tell her friend how to hopefully fix the situation that she'd gotten herself into.

"All right Bailey, go ahead and finish whatever it is that you wanted to say. I'm sorry that I kept cutting you off."

"No, forget it. You go ahead. I don't remember what I was going to say now," Bailey lied.

"Bailey, I know you didn't forget but fine. I'll finish. I'm always on your side when you're right, but when you know you're wrong, I'm going to tell you that too. And I'm sorry Bailey, but in this case you were wrong and you know you were. I've told you about a hundred times that Marcus is in love with you. And though he's pissed, he still is. You have been sending that man mixed signals from the very beginning. As a matter of fact, I told you that from the beginning that being with Marcus wasn't a good idea. Now at the risk of continuing to sound like a broken record, I'm going to get straight to the point.

"Good. It's about damn time," Bailey mumbled under her breath.

"Whatever. The point is, go get that man and stop being scared to take a chance on love or leave him the hell alone. And I mean completely. That means no more of this friend bull because you two have already had sex and have very deep feelings for each other. Stop thinking that you don't deserve to be happy. Stop being afraid to try something new. Fall in love again. I'm not saying that Marcus is without his fault, but from what you've told me, that man has put his heart on the line for you so many times that you've lost count. Newsflash love, that's love. Marcus has always wanted you. Stop making him work so hard at trying to prove to you that he's the one when he's done it ten times over already. Sorry for the tough love Bailey, but you were the one in the wrong in this situation."

"Maybe you're right." Bailey took a sip of her water.

"There's no maybe about it, you were wrong as two left feet."

"Oh and he wasn't wrong for acting like he was interested in Trina? Trying to make me jealous."

"Well it worked because you are jealous. I can tell that by the snide little way you said it. And y'all can be petty and play tit for tat if y'all want to, but all it's going to do is cause more problems and keep you two apart longer. Listen Bailey, life is too short for all this bullshit. If you love and want to be with that man, go after him. If the tables were turned, I'd have been made it crystal clear to anyone who would listen that he was my man. Now by no means am I telling you to settle, but I'm merely suggesting that you take a chance. Hell, close your eyes and just jump. Hopefully he'll be there to catch you when you fall."

******

The minute Marcus walked into Swivel Sticks, he regretted it. He wasn't in the mood to sulk with people around, especially when those people were coworkers, so as soon as he could, he turned on his heels and headed back out of the door. He had one foot out when he heard Trina call his name.

Refusing to turn around, he kept walking as if he hadn't heard his name being called several times. Pulling his phone from his shirt pocket, Marcus shuffled briskly to his car and prayed that Trina didn't catch up with him, but Jesus obviously didn't have time for him because even in six-inch pumps, she still managed to get to him before he got to his truck.

"Marcus?" Trina was practically screaming this time.

Shoving his cell to his ear, he whirled around and motioned for her with his index finger to wait one minute as he pretended to talk into his phone. As if he couldn't hear what the invisible person what saying on the other end, Marcus turned slightly and hurriedly turned the ringer off so the phone wouldn't ring while he was talking.

"Yes. I understand. Okay, great. Thank you so much. Exactly. All right, you bet. I'll see you in thirty. All right. You too. Goodbye." Pretending to end the call, he slid the phone back into his pocket and faced Trina.

"Hey Trina. I'm so sorry about that. I had to take that call."

"Oh no problem. I've been running behind you, calling you for quite a few minutes now."

"Wow, really? I didn't hear a thing. My mother's doctor was telling me some very crucial things about her health."

"No worries. I hope everything is all right though."

"It will be as soon as I get there. I'm on my way to take care of the situation right now actually."

"I was hoping that you weren't when I caught the tail end of your conversation, but I totally understand."

"Yeah, this thing can't wait," Marcus sucked his teeth as if he was truly disappointed.

"Right. I totally understand. Hey, maybe we could get together on our own time and grab a drink, and maybe even a bite to eat if you find the time, hopefully one day soon."

"Well, I'm always terribly busy, but I'll definitely keep you posted. But I really need to be going," Marcus pointed at his truck.

"Right. Oh no. I'm so sorry. Okay, go. And drive safely. We'll talk soon."

"All right, take care."

"You too."

Marcus jumped into his truck and took off as fast as he could down the street. Exhaling deep with satisfaction, Marcus laughed as he drove to his favorite dive bar, Honest Johns. He couldn't wait to get there and lick his wounds alone and drink his current mood away. He was ecstatic that he followed his first mind and made a U-turn right back out of that door at Swivel Sticks. It wasn't that he didn't like going for after work drinks and a side of trash talk with his coworkers. He'd done it many times before, in fact, but today he just wasn't interested, especially with Trina hanging on his every word behaving as if they were dating.

Usually he had Bailey there to keep Trina at bay, but by observing them all day, Trina knew something wasn't right, so she took that as her sign to pounce on him and sink in her claws. Though he knew what Trina had been trying to do, tossing a few back with the office sounded ideal at the time, but when it didn't make Bailey jealous and the more he thought on his impulsive decision, Marcus wasn't trying to go any further; plus, something in the back of his mind told him that it would be an extremely bad idea that he would live to regret.

Definitely think I dodged a bullet tonight. Poor Trina. She has got another thing coming if she thinks that there's ever going to be a chance for her and me.

Not in this lifetime or the next. Fortunately and unfortunately, the only woman I want is most likely somewhere with her ex making up for lost time right about now.

******

Zooming in with her Nikon D5500 to capture an up-close shot of a couple kissing stopped along the shade of the bike trail at Metro Beach, Bailey snapped several pictures of the happy couple before moving on to her next subject. Ambling around the beach, Bailey snapped pictures of everything that caught and held her attention. Taking pictures for both work and because of her love for the art, she'd been out capturing subjects for the last three hours. Though she didn't want to admit to herself, she was glad for the reprieve to focus on something other than Marcus and possibly Trina.

Just the thought of Trina hanging off of Marcus' arm at this very moment was enough to make her sick to her stomach, but she tried her best to behave as if she was unbothered. She was still trying to erase the image of seeing Trina snuggled up so close to him. It pissed her off to no end. Her only joy was that Bailey knew that Marcus had absolutely no interest in her and wanted nothing to do with her.

Well, unless he's changed his mind. After all, he is a man. And he doesn't have to find her attractive or even like her to spread her legs. Damn him for trying to make me jealous of that whore. And damn him because his stupid ass fake display worked.

Pouting, Bailey snapped for another half hour and then decided to call it a night. She was both mentally and physically exhausted. Between still trying to digest what Parker had preached and how she felt deep down, Bailey was nearly going insane–mostly because she didn't know how she wanted to feel.

Yes I do still have feelings for Cody. I wish I could help it, but I can't. Not all five years together were bad; only the last two. But then again, it could've been the entire time and I could've just found out when I did. Ugh, I swear I hate that I still love him, I don't really see us getting back together. I don't think. And hell, I don't know what to feel about Marcus. I've always loved him as a friend. And there was never any physical attraction. Well, at least on my part. But that has definitely changed now. Now it's like I can quite possibly have my man and friend all in the same person, but Marcus knows so much about me until I'm not so sure that that's a good thing.

I don't know how long our attraction to each other will last. Not that I don't know that nothing is guaranteed when it comes to love, I just don't know if I'm ready to take that chance. I don't want to hurt Marcus and I don't want him hurting me. He talks as if he's so sure that he won't, but I surely have my doubts. And one thing that I'm truly terrified of happening should we both decide to become more than friends is that Emily will come back and want a second chance with the man she was about to marry. Hell, how do I compete with that? And then there's all the women in his past that I don't know about. But I also know that those are all normal concerns when it comes to taking a chance on love. I guess I am truly just scared of loving him.

Chapter 20

"So what are you going to do, Marcus?" Anthony asked Marcus the million dollar question.

"I'm going to leave her the hell alone? What else am I supposed to do?"

"Do you want my honest opinion?" Anthony asked him as he devoured his second Coney at Lafayette Coney Island.

"Yeah, that's why I asked."

"All right, if you want her, go after her."

"Anthony, is that all the damn standard ass advice you have for me?"

"Pretty much," he laughed.

"Well thanks for nothing. You are absolutely no help whatsoever," Marcus sat back. The look on his face was somewhere between shock and disbelief.

"Just screwing with you, my friend. All jokes aside. You do need to go after her though. But go after her with everything. You need to lay all of your cards on the table, tell Bailey exactly how you feel. Tell her your secrets, tell her your fears. Come clean. Pull out all stops. Show her with words. Tell her how you've felt all along. How you wanted her while you were with Emily. Sit her down and hand her your heart. If she drops it, hey—just pick up the pieces and move on. It just wasn't meant to be. But if she takes it, finger it gently and place it close to her heart, then you got her. She's the one for you. It's not going to be easy but when it comes to love, those are just some chances that you have to take."

"Damn," Marcus mumbled as he pondered everything Anthony told him. He raked his fingers across his chin and jawline.

"What?" Anthony asked confused.

"Had a feeling you were going to say that."

"Okay, and what's so wrong with that?"

"I don't want to do it. It's not me... too personal. I'm a very private person. You know that."

"Well your private ass is going to just have to get used to being alone," Anthony chuckled.

"You're a prick," Marcus laughed.

"And I'll never deny that fact. But as long as you know I'm right then hey, I've done my job. And according to you, sounds like you better stop dragging your feet before you lose her. And the way your luck is going, it just might be to Jeremy," Anthony joked.

"Since you're suddenly a comedian now, see if one of them corny ass jokes get you back to your job," Marcus said as he stood.

"Hey, you know that was hilarious. And don't get mad at me because you're about to let another man steal your woman right out from under you."

"That'll never happen."

"Hey Marcus, who are you trying to convince? Me or you?"

******

When Bailey sauntered into her office and saw a dozen roses in a long white box opened on her desk, her hearted instantly melted. Closing the door behind her, she rushed over to them as she carefully pulled a card from its thorns. Closing her eyes, she hoped and prayed that they were from Marcus but when she flipped the card open, she was thoroughly disappointed because Marcus' name was nowhere on the card.

Hey gorgeous, hope you're having an amazing day and if you aren't, I hope that only flowers that come close to your beauty bring joy to your heart and a smile to your lips. Enjoy.

You're secret admirer.

Frustrated, Bailey placed the card back down, moved the flowers over to the windowsill, and glumly got ready to start her day. She missed Marcus terribly and wanted to go down the hall and tell him just that, but her pride nor her heart would let her. She felt that he should come to her first and apologize. She knew that she owed him an apology as well, but she had already made it up in her mind that she was not going to be the one to make amends first. As Bailey sat down to work, she hoped that he would give in and be the bigger person really soon, because them not speaking to each other and hanging out was pure torture, and as if them not speaking wasn't already annoying enough, her body was starting to crave him more and more.

Bailey tried not to think about sex at all, but with the way Marcus had made love to her, she was literally thirsting for a lick, touch, or at the very least a simple forehead kiss. Anything. She was bordering desperation and insanity if she didn't get a fix soon, and she didn't see that happening anytime soon with her and Marcus at odds.

Bailey had tried on many occasions since their friendship ended to pleasure herself with her many vibrators and other toys, but for the first time since she'd purchased them, they weren't bringing her to climax and on the few times they did, the feeling barely lasted.

"Ugh, what am I going to do? This makes no sense. Maybe I should just stop being petty and be the bigger person. After all, I guess I am the one who sort of started this by trying to push Marcus away. Looks like I've succeed too. But now I'd give anything to take that day back."

Temporarily pushing any further thoughts of her and Marcus out of her mind, Bailey hoped to numb her pain by completely drowning herself in her work. Refusing to let her focus wane, she struggled and fought with her sanity to stay on task and to lick her wounds later, and everything was going great until someone stopped him in front of her office to have a word with him. Flustered, Bailey pretended to still work diligently as she stood and eased closer to her door just to hear Marcus' voice. Leaning against the wall by the door, Bailey closed her eyes and listened to the slightly muffled deep timbre of his voice, and immediately her body betrayed her. Her nipples had become small mounds and her lower lips begin to pucker and throb with need.

"I miss that man so much."

Unable to resist the urge any longer, Bailey slipped hands between her thighs, and deep into her heat.

"Marcus. I miss you." Bailey widened her stance and propped one foot on her bookcase. Before she knew it, she was moaning Marcus' name a little too loud and only noticed because she could no longer hear the radio softly playing in the background or Marcus' voice.

"Gotdamn it, did he hear me?" Her eyes widened in horror.

Taking a deep breath, Bailey did her best to gather her nerves and as discreetly as she could be at this point, peeked around the door to see if Marcus was still just outside of her door. When she saw no one, she turned completely around for further inspection and breathed a deep sigh of relief when she saw that the coast was clear. Sliding back up against the wall for support, Bailey closed her eyes and shook her head.

Girl, you really need to get a grip.

Righting her skirt, Bailey went over to her desk, squirted a small amount of sanitizer into her hands, and headed back to the door.

I can't take this. I need to gather my thoughts and get some air.

Locking her door behind her, Bailey started down the hall toward the restroom. She turned right down another hall and was getting ready to turn left into the ladies room when she heard someone whisper her name, and before she could turn around, a hand went over her mouth and she could feel herself being pulled into the supply closet. Fear welled up in her and her heart beat hard against her chest as she struggled to break free from the strong grasp. Preparing to scream and fight as hard as she could when whoever's hand was currently covering her mouth, Bailey instantly calmed when the dim light flooded the dark room and Marcus' handsome face came into view. Once he visibly felt Bailey settle down, he placed his index finger to his lips and slowly moved his hand from over her mouth.

Exhaling when she realized that her life was no longer in danger, Bailey frowned, slapped Marcus across the arm, and turned to walk away.

"I don't know what the hell your problem is Marcus, but if you have something you want to say to me this is not how you do it." Bailey was almost to the door when Marcus grabbed her by the waist and pulled her back against his broad, massive abs and growing manhood.

"I'm sorry, but I'm not about to let you go." Marcus tugged and softly bit on the shell of her ear as his hands made his way between her thighs.

"Wh-what are you—"

"Hush Bailey and just enjoy the moment," Marcus whispered while brushing kisses down the back of her neck and shoulders.

Before Bailey could say another word, Marcus leaned Bailey over and slid inside of her drenched pussy from behind. As Marcus' strokes filled her, Bailey's soft moans grew louder and louder. Quickly, Marcus removed his tie and shoved it into Bailey's mouth to stifle her moans. When they were both satisfied with Bailey's muffled screams, which only seemed to heighten both of their pleasure, they both hungrily met each other, thrust for pound until bliss and pleasure shook them to their cores.

******

Marcus had. a hankering for something from the Orange Slice all week long but every time he would be ready to go, something would come up and he'd forget all about it, so as he prepared to leave the office, he phoned in his to-go order.

Organizing his workspace, Marcus took a seat behind his desk and began to search for his phone charger when his tie brushed against the side of his face. When he moved the tie, he was hit with a flashback of him and Bailey in the supply closet earlier. Grinning, he slouched back in his chair and locked his hands behind his head. His manhood had decided to join the trip down memory lane as he also saluted the memory.

Slowly, the memory and the moment faded and Marcus went back to searching for his charger. A few minutes later, he'd located it and after cleaning and prepping his workspace for tomorrow, Marcus went to turn off his lights and head out when someone slid a note under his door. Retrieving the note, he flipped it over and read the short message.

Marcus I've tried to be nice but I'm tired of being nice. I don't know what you see in Bailey, especially when I'm far sweeter and sexier, but some people just don't have good taste. My point is I want exactly what you gave Bailey in the supply closet, or I'm going to make both you and Bailey's lives a living hell. Starting with your jobs. And Marcus, if you think I'll just walk around making empty threats, please try me.

Love Trina.

"Fuck!" Marcus yelled as he angrily balled up the piece of paper and slammed it into the trashcan by his closet door.

Sliding a frustrated hand across his face, he continued to curse like a sailor as he paced his office, trying to decide the best way to handle this situation. Too livid to think right now, Marcus stormed out of his office and all the way to the parking structure. He was just about to take off and burn rubber as he sped down the street when he remembered his dinner order. He calmed himself as much he possibly could in this with Trina's threats treading heavily on his mind, and went to pick up his order.

Soon as he strode in, Sabrina met him at the door with his order.

"Hey handsome, you look like you've had a terrible day at work, so I personally prepared you order and made sure to have it in your hands so you wouldn't have to wait. So go ahead and enjoy your food. And you can call or stop in tomorrow and pay. Whatever it is, I truly hope it gets better for you. Have a good night Marcus. And enjoy the dessert." Before Marcus could respond, Sabrina headed back to work.

"Sabrina?" Turning around, she was strolling back toward him when he met her half way, picked her up, and hugged her tight.

"Thank you Sabrina. Thank you." Placing her back to her feet, Marcus kissed her on the cheek and left the restaurant, feeling slightly better than he did when he first walked in.

Chapter 21

As Bailey came around the track inside of the Fitness Adventures fitness center, she reveled in the beautiful fall scenery on the other side of the glass; gold, yellow, and burnt orange leaves falling from the now almost-empty branches and swirling around the cool, crisp afternoon air; soft, beautiful autumn sunrises casting perfect light down on the city; people briskly shuffling in this fall scarves, knit hats, and leather jackets.

Wow. What a beautiful scenery. I love the fall season. I still can't believe we'll be welcoming October in literally just a few days. It was just August. Bailey smiled warmly as she rounded the track again.

She went around another three times for a total of twelve laps. Jogging over to her locker by the sauna room, she took out her water bottle, sat down on the long bench, and gulped down the water as if she'd been roaming the desert all day. Once she had her feel, she grabbed up her belongings and headed home. She couldn't wait to get there to enjoy the rest of her day. Bailey loved her off days and couldn't wait to get home to finish enjoying it.

It wasn't even seven o'clock in the morning yet and she felt great. As she drove home, she nearly drooled on herself as she thought about her ham, cheese, and tomato omelet, turkey bacon, and breakfast potatoes with onions that she was going to prepare for herself as soon as she'd gotten home. Pulling into the Uptown market and grocery store around the corner from her house, she ran inside and grabbed water, cranberry juice, oranges, and grapefruit before finally pulling up to her home.

Grabbing her groceries, Bailey was sliding the key into the front door when the sound of a vehicle pulling up to her house caught her attention. Whipping around, she calmed when she saw that it was just her next-door neighbor.

Oh thank God. I thought that was Marcus and the last person I'm ready to talk to right now is him. It's bad enough that I see us in the supply closet every time I close my eyes. Not that it wasn't good, because it was absolutely amazing as always, but I just don't need to be thinking about him or how great he is as a person, or how quickly he gives me orgasms and how freaking fantastic he feels inside of me. I'm still pissed at him for the way he spoke to me and for ignoring me. But I can't stop thinking about him and wondering if he's doing to other women what he does to and for me.

Marcus not being in my life is pure torture. I don't know how much longer I can behave as if I'm okay with the way things are between us. But I still can't give him what he wants. I can't give him all of me. I'm just scared that I may not heal this time if I trust him with my heart. I just wish that I wasn't scared to love again, and I wish I no longer felt anything for Cody. Who knows, maybe one day I won't. Maybe one day I'll finally get this love thing right next time. But until then, I do still have my dildos and vibrators, and I love those guys very much.

Giggling to herself at her own joke, Bailey put her groceries away and headed straight for the shower. Undressing as she went along, she turned on the water, grabbed a washcloth, and was just about to step under the hot inviting stream when her phone rang. Hastily, she rushed into her bedroom and over to her dresser and without taking a minute to see who was calling, clicked the talk button.

"Hello. Hey beautiful!"

"What's do you want Cody?" Bailey rolled her eyes, but a smile tickled her lips because a very small part of her was happy to hear from him.

"Bailey, why do I have to want something? What can't I just call to see how you are?"

"Maybe because you've never done so before, so why start now?"

"Well people do have the right to change."

"Really, so you're saying that you're a changed man?" Bailey shifted her weight and sucked her teeth as she waited for him to respond.

"Yes, I'm a changed man. And this changed man would like to see you. So why don't you let me come pick you up at six tonight, and let's do dinner and a movie or something?"

"I don't know about all that, Cody. Besides, people don't change overnight."

"Well, how about you find out for yourself. Come on Bailey. Please? You know you miss me and that you want to say yes."

"Cody, just because I want something doesn't mean that I should have it."

"Come on woman. Loosen up a bit. Take a chance on me. You did before," he continued to try his best to persuade her.

"Please don't remind me. That is so not helping your case right now. But I guess it wouldn't hurt anything."

"Woman just say yes already."

"Fine. What time did you say again?" Bailey smiled.

"Six."

"All right. I'll see you at six."

*****

Marcus was in a bad mood. He had a million things running through his mind, and they all had to do with women. He was terribly horny for Bailey. Sabrina intrigued him, and he was ready to ring Trina's neck.

"Damn women, ain't nothing but trouble," he mumbled as he strode through his house slamming, kicking, and punching everything in his path. When he made it to his bedroom, he plopped down on his bed, closed his eyes, and attempted to come up with a solution to his little blackmail issue.

After about five minutes of frustration and annoyance, Marcus took a shower to scrub away the day before strolling into his kitchen to cook his way through his problems. A few hours later, Marcus had a huge spread including dessert spread out on his kitchen table. He'd prepared stuffed blue cheese crumbles and lobsters, sautéed rainbow trout, shrimp, zucchini, and tomato skewers sprinkled with garlic butter and chives, fried jumbo shrimp, cheddar cheese-twice baked potatoes, kale, and honey rolls. For dessert, he made red velvet cake, frosted carrot cake, and caramel glazed brownies.

Eyeing the spread, he grabbed a fork from the silverware drawer and made himself a sample plate. After pouring himself a glass of lemonade, he gathered everything and made himself comfortable on the couch in front of his mounted big screen television. He went to devour his plate when he suddenly glanced down at it, and realized that he no longer had a desire to taste the food. Taking a bite anyway, Marcus tried to focus on the television and ignore what was really bothering him, but it was no use; his life, his space, and even the food he cooked just didn't have the same flare without Bailey in it.

Placing his food on the table, Marcus sat back and closed his eyes. Right away, memories from the day the first met to their quickie earlier that day began to flood every crevice of his mind. Massaging his temples, Marcus wondered what Bailey was doing at that very moment, and if she was thinking about him.

"Why can't I stop thinking about her? Why do I crave her and why do I still care? How does she have me wrapped around her finger without even trying?"

Now with a taste for something stronger than his lemonade, he went and poured himself a Jack and just stared at the amber liquid through the glass before he snatched it up and slammed it down his throat. Gritting his teeth, he poured himself another and downed it in one swig before he was hit with an idea. Moving over to his cabinets above his sink, Marcus took down six Ziploc food storage containers and began filling them with food. Once all of the food he'd made was packed, he placed it in a big box, cleaned his kitchen, and rushed out of his house with the box in hand.

"I hope this works."

Chapter 22

Bailey didn't know when she nodded off, but when she woke up and glanced over at the time, she jumped up.

"No, how is it already five thirty? I just laid down," Bailey yelled as she jumped out from under her Egyptian comforter and ran to her closet.

Pulling out the green and black cocktail dress, she slipped it on. So happy that she'd showered before dozing off, Bailey rushed into the bathroom and finished getting dressed. After twisting her hair up into a bun, she applied light make-up to her face and once she blew her reflection a kiss, she went to her closet and began throwing one shoe over the other until she found her back stilettos with the sliver rim. She slid her feet into her shoes just as her doorbell rang.

Excited, Bailey jumped for joy and did a small victory dance on her way to the door.

"Just a sec," she sang as she scuttled through her house as fast as she could in heels.

Opening the door, Bailey couldn't contain her smile when she saw Cody on the other side looking like a million bucks. Dressed in gray and black from head to toe, the man oozed sex appeal.

Wow. So fine. Yes! Jackpot baby.

"Hello Cody," Bailey finally spoke. She was staring so long and intently that she'd forgotten to invite him in.

"Hello sexy. Can I come in?"

"Oh yeah. Sure. I'm so sorry come on in," Bailey's smiled widened when he walked past her, and his Burberry cologne almost brought her to her knees.

Goodness gracious, there ain't nothing like a good smelling man. But I have to admit, Marcus' scent is much more intoxicating and potent. Focus girl focus. Marcus is no longer in the picture. Beside, why are you even thinking about Marcus? Cody is the one you want, not Marcus. Right?

Shaking off the disturbing question she'd subconsciously asked herself because she wasn't sure if she knew the answer, she closed the door and moved into Cody's hug.

"You're looking amazing, are you ready to go or you need more time?" Cody asked.

"Um, let me go throw on some jewelry and grab my purse and I'll be ready to go."

"All right. Sounds good. Take your time." Cody kissed her on the cheek and took a seat on the couch. Running back to her room, Bailey opened her engraved jewelry box that her mother had given her for her 30th birthday; she slipped on her diamond studs, matching necklace and diamond bracelets, pulled down her black Coach bag from her purse rack on the inside of her closet door, and was back in the front room in under five minutes.

"Okay. I'm all set."

"Great. After you beautiful," Cody stood as they headed toward the door.

Fishing her keys from her purse, she got ready to hand them over to Cody so he could lock the door for her like he'd always done when she realized that she had the wrong guy.

It wasn't Cody who used to take the initiative and lock the door, it was Marcus. Damn it, how in the hell did I get them confused? Get it together girl, or next thing you know I'm going to be calling him Marcus. And then all hell is going to break loose.

After locking up and heading to Cody's car, Bailey suddenly couldn't stop thinking about Marcus and how she'd rather be with him right now. She toyed with the idea of canceling with Cody right now and going around the corner and just apologizing for everything, and talking him into making her dinner. She didn't think it would be in good taste to treat Cody like that though, so she dropped the idea all together, smiled a smile she didn't feel, and slid inside of the car.

"Bailey, is there something in particular that you have a taste for?"

"Huh? Um I'm sorry, what was that?"

"I said what did you have a taste for?"

"I don't know surprise me."

"Okay. I can definitely do that," Cody grinned as he happily headed off toward his favorite restaurant.

As her house became a speck in the rearview, Bailey once again contemplated dashing out on this date to spend the rest of the night laughing and watching old movies with Marcus, especially since she was finally ready to admit what she'd been refusing to acknowledge to herself—that she was falling hard for Marcus.

I'm in love with Marcus. Great, just freaking great.

******

Feeling damn good about his plan, Marcus climbed back into his truck after running into Mel's Corner Market, and drove back up the street toward Bailey's block.

"Hopefully, this bottle of her favorite red wine that I just went to three stores looking for it before I finally found it at Mel's and all of this food I made will at least get the crazy, stubborn little hot headed woman to open the door and talk to me."

Marcus didn't know how it happened, but he somehow drove right past Bailey's house, turning into the next available driveway, which happened to be three houses down on the left. Turning his head around as he backed out, he suddenly eased his feet onto the brake when he saw her coming out of her house, and when he saw that she wasn't alone and who was hanging on her arm, Marcus was furious. Balling up his fist, he slammed it into the steering wheel. As he sat there fuming, Marcus' first thought was to jump out of his truck and rearrange Cody's face, then shake some since into Bailey, but he quickly talked himself out of doing anything stupid and to wait until they drove off before he left.

"She wants to keep fucking with Cody's sorry ass excuse for a man. Then keep fucking the shady asshole. I'm done. I'm fucking done trying. Bailey, you want Cody, then by all means go for it. I wish y'all the motherfucking best."

Soon as Cody turned the corner, Marcus sped off and never looked back. He wasn't getting ready to admit it out loud, but he was hurt and he'd do anything not to be able to feel such a gut-wrenching pain that had just rocked his entire body. As he drove, he had no idea what his next move would be, but he did know that whatever it was, it would include a stiff drink, some good music, and the company of a woman. If he was lucky, whoever the lucky woman was about to be, she could be all night long.

Chapter 23

Causally sneaking glances at Cody as she sat in a cozy booth across from him at J. Alexander's on Big Beaver Road, Bailey wondered what she'd ever saw in Cody other than his good looks; because besides his outer appearance, he was a real self-centered jerk who thought that he could always throw money at a situation and the situation would be no more. As she continued to inspect him, she'd become disgusted with the man that he was. The real man; not the man who falsely presented himself as kindhearted, caring, and very selfless when it came to the woman he loved, but it was all a lie, because the more she got to see of Cody and the longer she stayed with him during their relationship, she realized that none of those things were true, and above all he was a liar and a womanizer.

What the hell am I doing here with Cody when I should be somewhere laughing at stupid shit with Marcus?

"Cody?"

"Yes beautiful?"

He didn't bother to even look up from his phone that had been ringing relentlessly and since they got in the car, and the entire time he made sure to keep his phone tilted toward him, so as not to reveal the woman's name Bailey assumed.

"Cody for Christ Sakes, please put the damn phone down for a second and listen to me, damn. I'm seriously starting to wonder if you meant to bring the chick that can't stop ringing your phone out tonight instead of me."

"Bailey, calm down baby. I just had to take care of a little business but I'm all done now. There is no other woman, only you. You know that you're the only woman for me," Cody smiled as he slipped his phone into his shirt pocket.

"Cody please. You're such a horrible ass liar." Bailey shook her head as she began to browse the menu.

"Baby, I'm not lying. And I really wish you believed me. I'm not that guy anymore. Trust me. I've turned over a new leaf. That last call really was business."

"Really, and what about the damn near hundred calls before that one?"

"Bailey baby, you're exaggerating. Not let's not argue please. Let's just enjoy the moment. I've missed you. You mean so much to me. Did you want to go catch a movie after this or go bowling after this?"

Hell no. I don't want to go anywhere else with you.

"No, I'm sorry. I'm going to have to pass tonight. I'm terribly sleepy and my head's been bothering me all day."

"Okay, well we can always go another day. How about we try again in a few days?"

"We'll see," Bailey said, though she had no intention going anywhere with him just as soon as the horribly boring date was over.

Bailey glanced up to grab her drink when she noticed a woman a few tables away quickly look away. At first Bailey thought nothing of it, but when she looked up and noticed the woman had done it again, she knew something wasn't right. Bailey was just about to ask Cody if he knew the woman, but his damn phone started going off again and when she looked back over toward the mystery woman, she was gone. It didn't take a genius to put two and two together.

Laughing to herself, Bailey slid her napkin from her lap, dropped it down on the table, grabbed her purse, and slid out of the booth.

"Cody?"

"Hold on baby. I'm going to go take this call and I'll be right—"

"Let me guess, you need the restroom? No, I need the got damn door," Bailey pulled out her phone and texted Parker, asking her to come and pick her up if she could.

"What, the door? Why?"

"Because I'm leaving. You have a nice life, Cody." Bailey's nonchalant expression let Cody know that she meant every word.

"Bailey. I don't understand. What's going on? What happened? I thought we were having a good time." He was puzzled.

This fool really don't get it. He's seriously trying to figure this shit out. He's not playing, he thinks I'm stupid in real life.

"Cody, why don't you ask the chick that you're texting? Wait, let me further clarify. Ask the chick that you were just texting–you know, the same one that was just sitting about three tables to your right. Well she's gone now, but I assume she's in the bathroom calling and texting you right now."

"Bailey, I swear it's not what you think. I- She is—"

"Cody, I don't want to hear the excuses. Let her know she can come on out the bathroom now. Goodbye Cody. Don't you dare ever contact me again."

The expression on her face this time was anything but nonchalant. Matter of fact, she was downright ecstatic as she sashayed out of the restaurant with the eyes of every hot-blooded man in the place glued to her every move.

******

Marcus sulked as he pulled back into his driveway. Cutting the engine, he got ready to open his door when he glared over at his front door and decided that he no longer wanted to step foot inside of his home any time soon. Revving his engine back to life, Marcus snatched his gear into reverse and sped away, as if he was fleeing from the devil himself. Forty-five minutes later, Marcus pulled into Gerald's Jerk Hut supper club. Between the Caribbean aroma, island spices of the Jamaican dishes, and the live reggae music that was coming from inside of the restaurant, Marcus was already starting to mellow out.

He was still pissed, but at least for the next few hours he could drown his anger and frustration in some good food and even better drinks. Since he visited The Jerk Hut regularly, he was greeted by both patrons and workers of the establishment when he walked in the door. As he returned all the genuine greetings, he ushered his way right over to his favorite booth between the bar and the stage, and took a seat. Before he even had a chance to get comfortable in the booth, his double shot of tequila was placed in front of him.

"Hey Marcus," said a beautiful waitress who was about 4'8 and truly easy on the eyes. Other than height, she was an exact replica of Janet Jackson in the movie Poetic Justice.

"Olivia, how are you? Thank you for my drink baby."

"I'm awesome, now that you're here. And anytime. You know that. Are you having your usual today?"

"Yes please. And could you please bring a coke and a water with my dinner please?"

"Absolutely. Everything will be up shortly," Olivia smiled as scurried off to the kitchen.

Taking in the smooth laid-back crowd, Marcus continued to let go of his grouchy mood and appreciate the view and the great sounds of reggae as it surged through his body. After making eye contact with several women in the club, he made a mental note to definitely get better acquainted with some of them when he saw a familiar face, a truly beautiful, angelic, familiar face that had just made eye contact with him and was coming his way.

"So I take it you're cheating on the Orange Slice for a little jerk huh?"

"Guilty as charged. Hello Sabrina."

"Marcus. I don't usually talk to traitors, but since their food is pretty damn fantastic here and since we sell two different types of cuisine, I guess you're off the hook this time," she joked.

"Thank you so much. I was really hoping for a pass."

"Perhaps today is your lucky day then."

"You know Sabrina, you just might be right," he smiled warmly at her.

"Well, I didn't mean to intrude. Please forgive me. I'll let you get back to your dining experience. See you around Marcus." Sabrina winked as she turned to head back into the direction in which she came, but Marcus cleared his throated and called out to her before she had the chance to disappear.

"Uh Sabrina?" Turning around when she heard her name, she smiled as she retraced her steps.

"Yes Marcus."

"You actually weren't intruding at all. In fact, it would really make my night if you would join me. If you're here alone, I mean."

Beaming, Sabrina bit her bottom lip as she slipped a few strands of her hair behind her ear before she responded.

"I'm actually not alone."

"Oh okay. My sincere apologies. I didn't mean—"

"But lucky for you, I'm just hanging out with family so they'll understand. So I guess I could join you. If you really want me to, that is?" Her smile was contagious.

"I really want you to."

"All right, but only under one condition?"

"Well, this just got interesting. And what might that condition be?"

"At some point before you leave, you must dance with me."

"You've got yourself a deal, pretty lady." Sabrina slid into the booth across from Marcus, and after having her food relocated to his table, they enjoyed a very animated, fun, and careful dinner.

The duo went on for hours talking, laughing, and just enjoying each other's company. The night ended up being a much-needed night out for the both of them. As promised, a couple of hours before closing, Marcus kept his word and they not only danced to one song, but ended up dancing the night away.

"Tonight is definitely going down as one of the best nights of my life," Sabrina sighed from joyful exhaustion.

"I agree. I had a great time," Marcus laughed as he walked Sabrina to her car.

"I'm glad you did, Marcus, but you know we could've done this a lot sooner. Why didn't you ever call? I waited for you those first couple of days. Do you already have someone special in your life?"

"I'll be honest, I really wanted to call, but I was dealing with something, or rather someone, when you reached out to me. So it was nothing more than bad timing."

"And now? Are you official with this someone now?"

"Official no. Not at all."

"But she is still around?"

"Something like that, yes. I'm currently trying to separate myself from this person, but I'm not sure how long that's going to take me. I like you. I really do. Was attracted to you from the first moment I saw you, but I just don't want to waste your time starting anything with you when I know that now just isn't a good time."

"I understand. And I really appreciate your honesty but I am a big girl Marcus. So whenever you feel like you're ready, I'll be looking forward to that call. Even if only for coffee."

"I'll definitely keep that in mind. You do that. Have a good night, Sabrina."

"You have a better one sexy."

Chapter 24

Drying her eyes with a couple of the wads of tissues that she had been crying into for the last five minutes, Bailey sat in the passenger seat of Parker's car relaying to her what just happened with Cody, and catching her up on what had been going on with Marcus.

"Damn Bailey, that is a lot to deal with, but you'll be okay in time sweetie. And at least one good thing did come out of all of this."

"No I won't. I'll never be okay," she sobbed.

"Yes you will and you know it."

"I don't know anything. And what's the one good thing out of all of this, because I'm failing to see it." Bailey dried her eyes.

"You've finally admitted that you're in love with Marcus. And that's one extremely big step in the right direction. Now all you have to do is let him know that you feel the same way about him that he feels about you."

"Yeah right. You know things are never that easy. The way my luck is going, some woman's going to see him and know what a great man he is, and snatch him up before I even get the chance to plead my case."

"Well Bailey honey bun, that's when you have to get your ass out there and beg and plead like an idiot, because you were the one who was wrong. Now if you want your man, girl you better go get his ass while this drama is still fresh between you two. Because if there is another woman, you're going to want to get a head start on this race before you finish last sweetie."

"Yeah I hear you, maybe you're right Parker. Maybe you're right."

"Oh you know I'm right. Now is not the time to play dumb. And just in case you've forgotten, a woman like Trina will get down and dirty and do whatever it takes to get the man she wants. So not only do you have to contend with the fact that there may be another woman lurking around, but if this Trina chick is anything like you described, then you have an entirely different set of issues to contend with, and if you don't believe me just watch. Mark my words, she'll stop at nothing. So like I said, you better get yourself together quick, because you are going to have to guess this woman's next move before she even thinks it up."

"Parker, you make this seem like some kind of competition for Marcus' love, and you know I don't compete without anybody when it comes to love."

"I understand all that, but remember you were the one who screwed up here. So know that you've realized you want Marcus and from that pitiful look on your face, don't want to live without him; you got to go plead your case. Make things right and get ready to get down with whatever woman that has her eyes on your prize."

"All right, you're right. And I hate it when your ass is right."

"Aww, I love you too girl."

"Whatever."

"So are you sure you want to still go home? Did you want to go run the town or something and talk strategy over good appetizers and even better cocktails?" Parker laughed.

"That sounds awesome, but I think I'm going to pass. How about we do that tomorrow night? I feel horrible right now. I just want to go home, curl up on my couch with my rum raisin ice cream, and watch the *Law and Order: SUV* marathon."

"I'll let you slide because I know exactly how you feel. But you get this sadness out of your system tonight because I don't want to see that ugly ass face tomorrow," Parker laughed.

"Shut the hell up. You're ugly when you cry too," Bailey laughed.

"I know, but we're talking about you right now," Parker continued to tease her as she pulled up to Bailey's house. Go cry it all out then fix yourself up. We got a town to take over, Pinky."

"I hear you Brain," she smiled. "Parker. Thank you so much for always being there for me. You're one hell of a friend." Bailey leaned across the seat and hugged her friend as if her life depended on it.

"Um, Bailey, you're so welcome but you're choking me," Parker pretended to wheeze, as if she was gasping for air.

"You're so extra. Thanks again. Bye. I'll call you later."

"Bailey, stop thanking me and get out of my car. I love you too." As soon as Bailey walked into her house, Parker drove away waving. Glancing around her home as he leaned up against the door, a smile tickled her lips.

It feels so good to officially be over Cody and to admit to myself that I'm head over heels for Marcus. But I'm nervous as hell that he's going to put me through the ringer as punishment. Shoot, I don't even know how to tell him, which is crazy because I used to be able to talk to that man about anything. I wonder what he's doing and if he's at home. Maybe I should call him and ask him if he wants to come over and watch a movie like he used to do. Ugh. I need to calm down first. Why am I so nervous?

"Screw this, I need wine," Bailey laughed nervously while pushing up off the door and moving into the kitchen.

Retrieving her favorite wine glass with her name engraved on it and her bottle of Serena's sweet red wine, she filled her glass and took a sip as she headed to her bedroom. Before she could fully darken her doorway, she was kicking off her pumps and letting her hair down. Sitting her wine glass on her dresser, Bailey undressed and slipped on a pink and white pajama shirt, and pink slippers before reaching for her glass. She continued to sip as she padded back into her front room. Clicking on the television, Bailey flipped to the USA television network and smiled when she saw Detectives Stabler and Benson of SVU appear on the screen.

"Now this is what I call a perfect way to end a night."

Quickly, Bailey made her way into the kitchen, grabbed her bottle of wine and the bag of tortilla chips and salsa, and danced her way back to her spot on the couch.

"Now, let's bring on the drama baby." Grinning, Bailey couldn't think of more perfect moment until her thoughts shifted and Marcus flooded her mind.

She missed him with every fiber of her being. She wanted to call him right now and ask if he wanted to stop by or if she could come over, but because things had been so awkward and strained between them lately, she felt that he would say no. The last thing she wanted to hear from Marcus right now was no– especially with her being so vulnerable right now. Her emotions were all over the place and her heart was just too weak to withstand any more pain. Since she'd made up her mind, she still leaned over her couch for her phone. Staring down at it, she unlocked it and scrolled to his name, then before she lost the nerve, she texted Marcus.

Hey, how are you? If you're free, do you think we could talk for a little bit when you get time?

There. I reached out to him. So if he doesn't respond, I won't ever bother him again. But I hope he responds. I really hope he responds. Please respond Marcus.

Laying her phone in her lap, Bailey waited on a reply when she suddenly became engrossed into the episode. By the time the first commercial came, she check her cell and nothing. She did that for the next few commercials and the next seven episodes of Law and Order, and still nothing. Feeling horrible for even trying, she sat her snacks aside, stretched out on the couch, and cried. No longer as interested in her show, she cried and cried and cried.

Wondering if she'd lost her chance at her last shot at true love, real love, Bailey decided to just accept her fate and live with the startling revelation that she was never going to get to experience true love. Shutting off her television and every light in her home, Bailey curled up into the fetal position and cried herself to sleep. Before her eyes became too heavy to bear, she promised herself that tonight would be the last night she could cry over anything having to do with love ever again.

******

For the rest of the week and the next few weeks that followed, unless it was work related, Marcus hadn't said one word to Bailey, and she hadn't had any words for him. Even their hellos had become so strained that they had avoided walking past each other all together. He'd almost came running to her side when he'd gotten her text, but he was sick and tired of her games, so he'd ignored her and went about the rest of his night like he'd never received a message. The next day though, he'd regretted it and wanted to talk to her; he wanted to know if the friend he used to have in her was still there.

Instead, Marcus suffered in silence, behaving as if nothing was bothering him. He missed their jokes, the movie nights, her falling asleep on him, and him doing the same. He missed cooking for her and seeing the almost sensual look on her face when she finally tasted the food. He missed holding her while she cried or when she was down. He missed it all and so much more, but was done trying to plead his case. He was done letting her wipe her feet on his heart, even though she didn't knew she was doing it in the beginning. What bothered him the most was when he finally confessed his feelings for and then did so repeatedly, and she blew him off.

At first Marcus planned to do whatever it took to make her see that he was serious and the she would always have his heart, but that rollercoaster lacked excitement really quick. Standing at his window, scanning the late afternoon view of the city, a part of him wanted to go down and ask all of the people hustling to and from their destinations their opinion of what he should do, and if he was wrong to ignore Bailey. He wanted a fresh perspective, but he knew that even if he were to go and take an opinion poll, it wouldn't matter because all that mattered was how he felt and he felt used, betrayed, and hurt.

Marcus also knew deep down that acting in anger and off his emotions in the spur of the moment wasn't going to make anything better, and he knew that he was really pissed off because Bailey wanted Cody over him, and he just couldn't fathom that. Marcus felt like Cody didn't deserve a woman like Bailey, and he was really jealous that Cody got and was probably still screwing over the woman who he knew that he would treat only like the queen she was.

Moving away from the window, Marcus got comfortable behind his computer and finished up his work for the magazine's next few issues. He gave himself a break from anything having to do with Bailey. Marcus had gotten through the rest of the day Bailey free, and he even waited until she left so he wouldn't run into her; he had succeeded at that too, but as he was packing up and getting ready to leave the office, there was a knock on his door that had changed all of that.

"Come in," Marcus said with his back to the door.

"Good God Marcus, how in the world do you manage to look so damn sexy without even trying?" Trina asked as she slipped her hands around his sides and up his chest.

"Trina, what the hell is your problem. Get the hell away from me." Marcus yanked her hands away from him and jumped back away from her.

"Oh come on Marcus, cut the act. You knew it was me," she laughed.

"Trust me, if I had I wouldn't have let your crazy ass in here. Now what do you want Trina, and you better make it fast before you turn around and find out that you're talking to yourself."

"I want you of course silly, and if I were you, I would really calm down on making threats and making demands when I can end your fucking career with my fucking pinky finger. You got that, or have you forgotten?" Trina's evil glare let Marcus know that she meant every word.

"For the last time, what do you want?" He'd just about reached his boiling point, and was getting ready to explode.

"To fuck Marcus. Your time is up baby. You are going to fuck me whenever I want for however long I want, or all the big wigs will have your little indiscretion in their possession in less than thirty minutes. I was going to make you bend me over now, but I don't like this aggressive side of you at all. So I'll just come back when you're in a better mood. And I swear, the next time your ass better be in a better mood. I mean, you better be standing in here with your dick in your hand. And it better be rock hard and ready for you to slide it right up into my pussy with no protection, just like you fucked Bailey. And oh, I just got a fantastic idea. I want that bitch to watch. So if you haven't filled her stuck up ass in, now is the time and you better remind her that if she tries to open her fucking mouth, that's her ass and yours. Bye baby. Have a good night. And smile honey, you looked pissed."

Chapter 25

Strolling into the Orange Slice to pick up her call-in order that she'd placed on her way out of the office twenty minutes ago, Bailey stood in the long line and patiently waited her turn. She had a long day and couldn't wait to get home, eat, and relax for the rest of the evening. On top of that, she was mentally exhausted from trying not to think about Marcus. Bailey was still hurt that he'd never responded to her text or tried to call her. It was so unlike him and between that and them barely speaking at work, getting used to his new behavior towards her was beginning to become a little too much for her. Huffing softly as the line began to pick up pace a bit, Bailey began to take in the restaurant surroundings and a small smile appeared on her lips.

Wow. This place has such a homey feel. Maybe I'll just have my dinner here and sulk in silence instead of licking my wounds at home.

Bailey continued to take in the homey place with its deep orange and white orange-sliced decal-dressed walls, and cozy mahogany and white love seats that matched the tables. While continuing to scour around for a possible place to sit should she decide to stay, she didn't find a free table but as the line moved, she was able to see more seating along the side and back of the wall. Grinning inwardly, Bailey was next and she was just about to let the cashier know that she was staying when glanced to her right for a tray, and saw Marcus with the owner of the restaurant in what seemed to be an intimate conversation as he held hands and rubbed her loving on her back.

Before she could be seen, Bailey snatched her credit card from her wallet, paid her for her food, and swiftly moved through the exit. Once in her car and out of sight of onlookers and Marcus, she broke down. As she cried, she put two and two together and came to the conclusion that that's why Marcus never returned her text and called to see what she wanted.

"He was acting so unlike himself, so distant, and that woman in there is why. He really doesn't want me anymore. I can't believe I pushed him away," Bailey cried.

Reaching into her back seat for her emergency box of tissue, Bailey dried her eyes as best she could as more tears fell, and was just about to start her car head home when spotted the two of them walking out of the restaurant together. Bailey watched as Marcus pulled Sabrina into his tight embrace before he finally, but very slowly let her go.

Sabrina waved goodbye to Marcus and he walked back toward the office, seemingly too distracted to notice his surrounding because if he had, he would have noticed Bailey's forlorn expression following his every move until he disappeared into the parking structure. Feeling miserable, Bailey slowly pulled her car in reverse, carefully backed out, and drove home. When she finally arrived home, she kept her glum demeanor as she walked with her head down through the door. Placing her food on the kitchen counter, Bailey traipsed into her room, fell onto her bed, and wept into her pillow until the sunlight was replaced by the moonlight.

******

Scrounging her face up in pain when she felt as if someone was repeatedly striking her on the side of her head, Bailey carefully sat up and cradled the side of her head and face as the pain intensified. Slowly she opened her swollen, puffy bloodshot eyes and began searching her room for her bottle of Bayer aspirin. When her search came up empty and it finally dawned on her where her painkillers were, she groaned in pain. Taking a deep breath, Bailey slipped her feet into her house shoes and stood, and made her way to the bathroom. Opening the medicine cabinet after switching on the light, she popped two of the white pills into her hand and swallowed them dry.

Taking in her reflection when she caught a glimpse in the mirror, Bailey turned away in disgust. She was so disappointed in herself for letting her emotions overtake the way she did.

Never again will I do this to myself.

Bailey shook her head as she entered her kitchen. Washing her hands, she poured herself a glass of water, gulped it down, grabbed her carryout, and put it in the microwave. Twenty minutes later, she sat down at her kitchen table to her Orange chicken, steak chunk, and vegetable stir fly with a tall glass of papaya juice. She ate in silence as she pondered her life and relationship goals. Other than becoming a world-renowned photographer, she was happy, but her life seemed to be one disaster after another.

I want to be happy; happy in love. Why is it that I can't find love? Why is it that I keep choosing the wrong damn men? I'm so tired of pulling my heart on the line, thinking it'll be different this time. When am I going to luck up and find the one for me? Shit, I'm really starting to believe that real love don't fucking exist or that it's just not for me. Guess I better just get used to being alone because I'd rather be alone than settle like I have so many times in the past.

I'm so scared to love, but I want to be loved genuinely. I want those late night talks, that slow lovemaking under the stars, taking spur of the moment road trips just because, and random roses and texts because he's thinking about me and so much more. I want it all. I deserve it all, but me being happy in love just isn't meant to be. It's crazy, I never in a million years would've pictured my love life like this. Nonexistent. Ha! And I got the damn nerve to be a damn hopeless romantic. Love sucks ass. Think I'll go get a couple of cats tomorrow, since I'll be an old maid.

Doing a horrible job at trying to cheer herself up, Bailey placed the rest of her food into the refrigerator and was getting ready to go park herself in front of her big screen when she realized that right now, she'd rather be anywhere but home wallowing. She jumped in the shower, threw on her workout clothes, and drove to the twenty-four hour gym two blocks away from her house.

From here on out, I'm done with hoping for and believing in love. I just want fast and hard quickies so I don't have to worry about a broken heart, plenty of ice cream and wine or wine-flavored ice cream— whichever I'm able to get to first—and lifetime movie marathons. Fuck love and everything that has to do with it. Never again will I let the words I love you make their way between my lips. Never will I allow myself to ever be that vulnerable again.

****

Marcus was consumed with irritation and had been ever since Trina made her little threat. While he'd concluded that it was just easier to give Trina what she wanted and go ahead and screw her brains out, he wasn't in the business of conceding to the demands of people who thought they could control him by the dirt one had on him. He'd been mulling over ways to beat Trina at her own game. Pacing, he reflected on past conversations to see if she'd told him anything he could use against her. He immediately became annoyed when he couldn't find anything.

Think Marcus, there has to be some kind of way to beat her at her own game.

Casting a glance over to the clock, Marcus wondered what time Trina was leaving the office today. Just when he was about to go inquire around the office, she came rushing past his office down the hall to the copy room. Reaching across his desk for his coffee mug, he was on his way out of the door when he saw that another note had been slid under his door. Staring down at the note, he sat his cup in his bookcase and wished that he had special powers to see through it so he wouldn't have to pick it up. Annoyed with himself for continuing to stare down at the folded piece of paper like it was going to open itself and jump into his hands, Marcus grabbed up the note and read it.

Hello you sexy beast. Change of plans. I'm headed out of town on a family emergency but I will be back bright and early Monday morning. So you get a few more days to plan exactly how far you want me bent over your desk and anything else you want me on. Oh, I can't wait for you to take me over and over again. It's going to be so good. Well, I have to run. Rest well and do whatever you have to do to keep your stamina up, because you're definitely going to need it.

Until Monday my sweet. Keep it hard and I'll keep it wet.

   Trina aka your freak.

   Scouring up his face, Marcus angrily balled up the piece of paper and tossed it in the trash.

   "Crazy ass broad, thinks she's going to blackmail me into giving her some dick. She's got another fucking thing coming if she thinks she's going to punk me into this bullshit."

   I'm going to find a way out of this shit, but I need to do it fast and I'm going to need help. But just in case whatever plan I come up with fails, I need to let Bailey know that her job is in danger too, right? No, the less she knows, the better. She's a damn worrying ass. Plus, it'll be kind of awkward for me to just drop by or pop up by like we're old friends. But I had no business just dropping by anyway; guess I've just gotten used to it. I'm going to have to call her first and ask if it's all right for me to stop by. Because I have to do that now, it really annoys the hell out of me. Whether it's in person or over the phone, Bailey is the last person I want to see right now, especially since she's back with Cody's weak ass.

   Sighing with contempt, Marcus exited his office and moved down the hall to Bailey's office. He got ready to knock on her door, but stopped short when he began to have second thoughts about talking to her about this at work. Backing away from her door, he heard Jeremy's almost sinister-like laugh behind him.

   "Bailey's not in, she went to grab us lunch. But I'd be happy to take a message for you though." He shrugged his shoulders and moved in front of her door as if he was guarding it.

"I'm good Jeremy. Thanks for being so concerned. That's cool of you. Anyway, bro I'll see you around." Marcus saluted Jeremy and walked off chuckling as he shook his head.

"Fucking prick. If only dude knew."

Pulling out his cell, he scrolled his call log for Bailey's name and hit the talk button. Immediately, he was greeted by her voicemail. Ending the call, he tried again and again, the same thing happened. After a third time, Marcus had a feeling that Bailey was intentionality sending him to voicemail. He called again and it was confirmed, he was again sent to voicemail.

"Great. Here we go. I'm going to have to tie Bailey's ass up just to get her to hear me out. But then again, tying her up just might work."

Chapter 26

Bailey had just dressed in a spandex, crop tee and yoga pants when there was a knock at her door. Walking over to her door, she glared out the peephole and her breath caught.

My oh my, why does this man get sexier and sexier every time I see him? But what the hell is he doing here? He knows I don't like people just popping up unannounced at my damn house. Shit, he could've called first. Oh wait, he did and you sent him to voicemail. Well so what. I called him weeks ago and he never responded. So I gave his ass a taste of his own medicine. I'm extremely curious as to why he's here though. And if he thinks that I'm about to let him in, then he's got another thing coming.

"What do you want Marcus?"

"We need to talk. Please open the door."

"We have nothing to talk about Marcus. Now go away."

"Bailey, I'm not going anywhere until we talk."

"Well have fun out there on the porch then. Goodnight."

"Bailey?"

"I said good night Marcus." Moving away from the door and into the kitchen to start her dinner, Bailey rolled her eyes.

He has got some nerve. He wouldn't even respond to me and thought I was about to open my damn door. Ha! And he better get off my damn doorstep before I go tell the police. Shoot, let me go tell him that right now.

She was on her way back to the door when she heard him calling her name as he came down the hallway from her bathroom. Bailey was so startled that she ran smack into the closet door and fell to the floor.

"Bailey, are you all right?" Marcus rushed to her side and scooped her up into his arms, and carried her over to the couch.

"Get the hell off of me. Let me go Marcus." Bailey scurried out of his lap and cowered over into the corner of the couch. "How in the hell did you get in here Marcus?" Bailey yelled while holding the side of her face that hit the door when he surprised her.

"Though the bathroom window that I told you needed to be replaced."

"Get out now Marcus."

"Bailey, I'm not going anywhere other than to get you some ice for that knot that's forming on the side of your head," he said as he stood, removed his sweater, and strode in the kitchen. Retrieving the ice and a hand towel, he moved back to Bailey's side and held the homemade compress to her face. Snatching it away from him, Bailey moved over to the other couch and eyed him menacingly as she stretched out and held her ice to her head.

"Bailey please let me—"

"Marcus you can't do anything for me but get the hell out of my house."

"I feel horrible, let me hold you and the ice for you please. It's the least I can do." His heartfelt plea was slowly inching its way into her heart.

"No, the least you can do is leave me alone. We have nothing else to say to one another."

"That's not true."

"It is so." Smiling, Marcus nodded.

"All right, I'm tired of going back and forth with you."

Moving over to her, he kicked off his shoes and crawled onto the couch, and pulled her into his arms. Grabbing the compress from her, he held it to her head.

"Now Bailey, we can do this the hard way or the easy way. You can let me hold you until the bruise on your face goes down, or I can tie you down and make you listen to what I came to tell you. What's it going to be?"he whispered into her ear while sliding her hair from her face.

Bailey hated to admit it, but she wanted to keep up a fuss so he would tie her down. She missed him so much–his touch, his smell, the way he kissed, and the way he locked eyes with her. It was so unnerving and sexy. Making sure to avoid eye contact with him, she continued to turn her head away while Marcus kept gently turning her chin toward him, while she silently begged her body to get a grip and calm down. Her overactive hormones weren't trying to hear anything she was saying though. Her nipples were standing at attention, begging to be sucked, and her clit was throbbing. Every time her thighs touched, she would become excited.

Resist him. Take control of your body before you end up spreading your legs to him and riding him for the rest of the night.

"You're awfully quiet all of a sudden, what's the matter? You want me to tie you up, don't you?" A sly grin slid across Marcus' lips.

"No I don't. I don't want you to do anything to me. Now please let me go." Bailey's voice shook when his hand brushed her side.

"Well from the looks of your nipples begging me to slide them into my mouth, I'd say you were lying."

"I'm not—"

Before she could say another word, Marcus pulled Bailey's bra down and slid one of her fat peaks in between his lips.

"Ohh Marcus. Please."

"Please what?" He smiled around her nipple before sucking it into his mouth.

"Um, please don't—"

"Fine. I'll stop, for now." He kissed her breasts and let her bra fall back into place.

"No, I didn't mean for—"

"You didn't me for what, Bailey?" Marcus moved his hand down her thighs. He purposely grazed her pussy lips before resting his hand on her stomach.

"Nothing. Never mind. Just tell me what you want, whatever you're here to say, and get out," Bailey huffed in frustration.

"You sure?"

"Yes, I'm—

Bailey's words remained stuck in her throat when Marcus slipped a hand in her pants and palmed her bare ass before running his hand along her pussy lips and slowly slipping two fingers inside.

"Marcussssss!"

"Yes Bailey?"he grinned, removed his hand, and slid his soaked fingers into his mouth.

"Don't do this to me," she moaned softly.

"Do what?"

"Okay stop. Thank you for holding the ice pack for me, but I'm good now. Can I go sit on the other couch please?" Bailey tried to calm her horny raging body, but realized that it was too late; she was on fire, and only Marcus could put out that fire.

"I'd rather you didn't but if you insist—" Quickly, Bailey jumped up and went to the other couch.

"Whelp, I guess I'll just go ahead and tell you why I'm here."

"Yeah, that would be a good idea."

"Right, well uh do you remember the day I pulled you into the supply closet and put my d—"

"Yes. Yes Marcus, I remember. Get to the point please."

"Trina heard us and she's blackmailing us. She says she's taking the tape to headquarters unless I screw her like I did you in the closet and anything she wants."

"What?"Bailey sat up and threw the compress across the room.

"Bailey I'm—"

"Marcus, that's my fucking job. You put my fucking career on the line. I knew your horny ass was going to get us in some deep shit." She hopped up and began pacing in front of him.

"How could you?"

"Bailey, I'm sorry. But I didn't hear you putting up a fuss while you were trying to keep from screaming my name."

"Marcus, now is really not the time to be a smart ass." Bailey rested her hands on her hips and frowned. "You know exactly what I mean. And how did I get dragged into the blackmail part?"

"Guilty by association, I guess."

"That's so like that bitch, and it's fucked up but you got to do what you got to do," she shrugged.

"Bailey I'm not doing it."

"The hell you're not. This is our lives the twisted trick is toying with. You screw her and you do it good."

"No. And she wanted me to do her with no protection."

"That's fucked up too, but this has nothing to do with me. Please don't put my career on the line Marcus."

"Listen I have a plan. So don't worry. Everything will be fine."

"A plan?" Bailey whipped her head around and stared him as if he were insane.

"Yes, we have to find some dirt on her so we can keep our jobs and she loses hers."

"And what exactly did you have in mind, Marcus?"

"I don't know yet. I'm still pondering."

"You're still pondering. You're still fucking pondering? Of course you are. Shit. Please tell me that this isn't happening." Bailey threw her hands up in disappointment.

"Bailey, just calm down," Marcus chuckled.

"Marcus, I don't see shit funny about this situation."

"It's not funny but—"

"You've already screwed her, so why are you suddenly so against it now?"

"Bailey, I've never didn't anything with her ever."

"What about that day—"

"Never." Marcus stood and walked up to her. Bailey backed up until she was trapped between Marcus' broad chest and the wall.

"I don't believe you Marcus."

"Well believe it. The only pussy I was sliding my dick inside of was yours. And as soon as you quit playing games and acting like a fucking child, I'll happily give you a ride down memory lane," Marcus whispered in her ear.

Before Bailey had a chance to say anything else, Marcus picked her up, braced her against the wall, and kissed her so thoroughly until she had no choice but to enjoy the ride.

Chapter 27

Marcus was having an extremely hard time containing himself. He wanted Bailey bad, and he had no idea how much longer he was going to be able to behave. To hold, kiss, and taste her after what seemed like forever was really doing a number on him. He wanted to tease Bailey, but his plan to get her to come to him was beginning to backfire.

No, she wants Cody. Don't let her use you. Move on.

Though it took everything in him to let go, Marcus placed Bailey back onto her feet and ended the intense kiss. The need and desire that filled her eyes was enough to push him over the edge, but he had to muster some kind of control so they could come up with a way to reverse the blackmail. Marcus also wanted to remind Bailey just what she was missing. He didn't care about making her come because she belonged to someone else now, but he wasn't going to do anything with her until he had her begging him to fuck her.

"So are you going to help me take care of Trina?"

"Are you admitting that you need my help?"

"I'm saying that I would like your help."

"Yes. I'll help you Marcus. That's what friends are for." A small smile began forming at the corners of her perfectly full lips.

"Oh, so we're friends now huh? You sure your man is cool with that?" Marcus smirked. He brushed past her and headed into the kitchen.

"What are you talking about, Marcus?" Bailey asked as she followed him.

"Cody." He grabbed one of the beers he left over in the fridge and gulped it down.

"Cody?

"Are you suddenly hard of hearing?"

"Cody's not my man. What makes you think—ohhhh, I get it. It all makes since now. You saw us that night and you came to your own little stupid ass conclusion. You hurt your own damn feelings. That's why you've been treating me like shit. Listen Marcus and listen good, Cody is not my damn man. He asked me out and I agreed. I wanted to see exactly what it was about him that I still cared for and if I still had any type of feelings left for him. Come to find out, even though I'll always care for him, there's nothing there. I gave him a piece of my mind and left his ass at the restaurant as soon as we got there and that was that. All you had to do was ask. I would've told you. You know that."

"You're telling the truth, aren't you?"

So I've been an angry jackass toward her for nothing?

"I have no reason to lie to you, Marcus," Bailey shook her head in disbelief. "Do you see what happens when you assume? You make an ass out of yourself," Bailey laughed.

"I'm sorry Bailey. I feel like a total ass."

"Hey, forget about it. But you owe me big time for treating me like crap though."

"Yeah I guess I do." He walked over to her and pulled her close. "You have any ideas on how I could make it up to you?" Marcus asked while placing soft pecks along her neck and shoulders. Smiling, Bailey pushed him back and began to back up.

"Oh I don't know, you said something earlier about tying me up?" Bailey winked and bit the inside of her bottom lip.

"Yeah, I might've said something along those lines. Why?" he chuckled.

"Well, where's the rope?" Bailey continued to back up.

"You know, I was going to bring rope but then I remembered how much you liked my ties soooooo—" Marcus pulled four ties from his jacket pocket and smiled. "Are you ready to be tied up Bailey?"

"Only if you can catch me first." Bailey took off down the hall, thinking that her head start would buy her some time, but Marcus was right on her heels and as soon as she glanced back to see how much distance she had on him, Marcus had grabbed her up into his strong arms, carried her to her bed, and gently laid her down in the center.

"You know you're in trouble, right?"

"Yeah, but exactly how much trouble?"

"Enough to keep you coming on my tongue and dick until morning.

******

Bailey was on cloud nine and still floating. Last night with Marcus had given her a total jump start. She couldn't contain her joy. When Marcus made love to her last night, he managed to touch her body, mind, and soul. She felt as if she'd just been cleansed. His kisses, the way he tongued both of her lips, was so refreshing and mind blowing until she'd actually skipped into work this morning. Just reliving some of their scandalous late night and early morning moments of ecstasy had her wet and ready, just waiting for Marcus to slide inside of her.

He had me coming all over the place, and the way he tied me up and ate my—

"Fuck this. I can't take this anymore. I need to come again right now." Pulling her vibrator from her purse, Bailey spread her legs and slid a finger inside of her, toying with her pussy until she could no longer control herself anymore. She slid her vibrator between her lips and was getting ready to slide it completely inside of her when a knock sounded at her door.

"Damn it. No. Not right now. Come back later please. I need to come so bad right now," she silently whined. Glancing toward the door, Bailey took a moment to decide whether or not she wanted to open her door and have her moment shot to hell but after further contemplation, she thought it best to let whoever it was in, just in case it was important. After all, she was supposed to be working.

"It's open."

Realizing she still had her vibrator in her hand, she quickly shoved it into her desk drawer and waited for whoever it was to come barging in but after a moment or two passed and still nobody opened the door, she hunched her shoulders and went back to work. When there was a knock a second time, Bailey pushed back from her desk and went to see who needed a hearing aid.

"Whoever this is better have a good damn reason for disturbing me," she mumbled.

Opening the door, she got ready to spout out a sarcastic greeting only to find that there was no one standing on the other side. Poking her head out of her door, she looked left and right but found no one. She was just about to close the door when she saw a small, white partially opened box propped against the wall with her name on it. Again, she glanced around but found no one. Retrieving the box, Bailey closed the door and began to inspect it. Peeking inside, she found a small jewelry box and a folded note. Curious as to what was in the jewelry box, Bailey opened that first to find a beautiful diamond tennis bracelet.

"Wow. This baby is gorgeous. But why would someone give this to me?"Placing the bracelet back into the box, she opened the note.

My love. I hope you enjoy the gift I purchased for you. Please slip it on and come around to the copy room for the ultimate gift. Me. Today I reveal myself to you.

Love, your secret admirer.

Expelling a deep breath, Bailey grabbed the box and headed out of her office.

"All right, finally. It's time to get this foolishness over once and for all."

Rounding the corner, she went into the copy room and stopped short when she saw a single rose with her name written on a card laying across it.

Moving toward it, she picked up the note. At the bottom of the card, she followed the single word at the bottom on the card that read *over,* and did as she was told. After flipping it over, the words *look up* caused her to immediately turn toward the door.

"Hello Bailey."

"Jeremy?"

"The one and only baby. Are you ready to ride off into the sunset with your knight in shining armor?" He laughed as he began to pose.

"Jeremy, what are you doing? And what the hell are you talking about? Wait, are you responsible for all of this? You're my secret admirer?" Bailey was instantly annoyed. She'd planned to let her admirer down easy, but with Jeremy she wasn't going to be as gentle with his feelings because not only wouldn't he accept no for an answer, he was always trying to throw his money at her just to get her attention. She'd tried to let Jeremy know many times that while she appreciated his admiration, she just wasn't interested.

"I am. I'm guessing you knew it was me all along, huh beautiful?"he grinned.

"No, I didn't know. But Jeremy I've told you a million and one times that we could never be because I am just not interested. Here, take your bracelet and I have all of the rest of the gifts you've given me in my office, except for the food. I tossed it because I had no idea who'd sent it. Please come get your things from my office and please respect my decision. I am just not interested."

"No, you go ahead and keep the gifts. But I'm curious. If I'm not your type, who is?"

"Jeremy why does that matter?"

"Because I'm just wondering if Marcus is more your type, or if you just make it a habit of screwing random guys in supply closets?"

"Excuse me? First of all, you're out of line. And secondly, you have your facts mixed up." Bailey was fuming. She was trying her best not to shake with nervous anger.

How the hell does he know? Does the entire office know? Oh my God, they know. They have to know. How else would he know?

"No Bailey, I don't. You and I both know that I'm talking nothing but facts here. And thanks to Trina, I've got the tape to prove it."

"You don't have a damn thing on me." Bailey looked up at his face in total disgust.

"Bravo, your acting is quite convincing, but we both know that I'm not hardly the one who's bluffing here." A smile slid across his lips that was almost sinister.

"I have no idea what you're talking about. Now get the hell out of my way," she spat with fury.

"No problem," Jeremy stepped aside. "But before you go, let's cut the bull. I'm putting the same offer on the table as Trina has with Marcus, which is basically saying that you're now my sex slave. You belong to me and have to spread your legs to me anytime I want, or Trina and I go to headquarters. You've got until Monday to give me an answer. And I know you're not stupid so starting Monday, I only want to see you in thongs, and they better match your bras or I will paddle that sexy ass of yours. Enjoy the rest of your day,

Bailey. And by the way, I had lunch ordered for us. Feel free to join me for a private dining experience."

Chapter 28

Marcus had just stepped onto the elevator on his way down to the cafeteria when Bailey came rushing up behind him into the elevator just before the doors closed.

"Hey sexy. You looking for a quickie?" Marcus brushed up against her and softly blew on the shell of her ear.

"No Marcus listen, I have to tell you something. I just—"

"Meet me in the supply closet. Bring that ass, I'll bring the tie." Marcus walked up behind her and pinched her on the behind.

"Marcus, listen please. This is serious."

"All right I'm sorry, but you can't blame me for not being able to keep my hands off you. Last night just wasn't enough. I need more. Come back to my office with me and sit on my face."

Under normal circumstances, his grin would've been her undoing, but right now there was a more serious matter to tend to.

"Marcus," Bailey pouted and stomped her feet.

"All right, what's wrong? I got sidetracked again. But you shouldn't look so good. But I'll give you give you two minutes. After that I can no longer be responsible for where I put my hands or my—"

"It's Jeremy," she said just as the elevator doors opened.

"Bailey, do I have to go beat his ass?" The scowling look on his face was almost menacing.

"No. I mean maybe. Wait, I'm jumping the gun." Bailey wrung her hands in panic.

"Bailey, what the hell is going on?"

"He knows. Jeremy knows about the supply closet. He teamed up with Trina and he's blackmailing me too now. He wants the same thing Trina wants," Bailey continued as they rounded the corner to the cafeteria.

"Okay listen, don't worry about it I—"

"Marcus, what do you mean don't worry about it? They are going to--"

"Bailey. What I was trying to say before you cut me off was not to worry because I'll take care of it. I'll go talk to him tonight. Trust me, everything is going to be fine," he stroked her arm assuredly.

"I'm sorry, I just don't believe that. And we still haven't come up with a way to make Trina back off. This is serious. This is our lives their playing with here. I just—"

"Bailey, I'm going to take care of all of this, but you have got to trust me. You've got to believe in me. Can you do that please?"

"I can try."

"Well baby, then that's good enough for me."

******

Bailey was leaving the mall from taking herself on *a just because you deserve it* shopping spree when her cell rang. Fishing it out of her back pants pocket, she answered without really paying attention to the screen.

"Hello."

After first there was silence, but just when she was about to hang up, she heard moans. Familiar moans. Her moans and Marcus' grunts of pleasure as he plunged into her repeatedly in the supply closet. Wide eyed, she snatched her phone away from her face and read the screen. Though the screen read unknown caller, Bailey knew exactly who it was and it was confirmed when Trina began laughing hysterically before she eventually hung up. Staring at the phone, she was instantly enraged.

"All right Trina, you want to keep crossing lines. Fine, let's go. You think you got me by the throat; well I'm about to show you something."

Picking up the pace, she walked briskly to her car, jumped inside, made a call, and sped off. Twenty minutes later, she was pulling up to Parker's house. As soon as she got to the door, Parker was greeting her.

"Hey."

"Hey Parker."

"Go upstairs Bailey. I was putting up my new bedroom set when you called." After Parker locked the door behind them, she grabbed a bottle of Italian sweet wine and two wine glasses before she joined Bailey in her room.

"Now what in the world has got your panties all knotted up?" Parker said as she filled their glasses.

For the next two hours, Bailey told Parker everything about her current dilemma, and caught her up on some things that she'd been meaning to tell her.

"Damn. You've just been running around here starring in your own little reality show huh?" Parker laughed.

"Parker cut it out. Ain't nothing out this mess funny," Bailey pouted.

"The hell it ain't." Parker's laughter continued to fill the large room.

"Whatever. I can't stand you Parker."

"Hey, don't get mad at me because you've been bouncing up and down in closets, oh and in parks too," Parker shook her head in total amusement.

"Says the one who was bent over roof tops, fire escapes, and restaurant bathrooms" Bailey eyed her knowingly.

"Hey, I was helping out with a state wide survey. So you cannot bring any of that up to support your point."

"What about the time in the bushes at your aunt's house?"

"Fine, point taken. But this isn't about me and you being jealous of my extracurricular activities. This is about you. So what's your plan, are we going to beat some ass? Because you know, I'm always down for that."

"No, not yet. I was thinking something more permanent."

"Bailey, it doesn't get more permanent than an ass whopping."

"I know, but I want something that will screw her out of her job, like they're trying to do us. I need you to ask your cousin to hack into her computer and social media accounts, and her cell if possible. And I hate to say this, but I need him to put a rush on it."

"Okay, I'll call Charles as soon as he gets off this evening."

"Cool. Thank you. Tell him to call me so we can talk about a price."

"Bailey, don't play with me, you know Charlie don't want no money. You know he's going to want a date."

"Yeah, but that thing he had for me was so long ago, hopefully the money will be enough."

"Well then you better guess again, because he still has the hots for you. He still asks me about you quite regularly, as a matter of fact."

"Really, how come you never told me that he still inquires?"

"Because since you've fallen in love with Marcus, you haven't been able to see past him to anyone else. So what would have been the point?"

"Yeah, you're right."

"But now he's definitely going to want something in return, and you know it."

"Well hopefully as my best friend, you can help me out," Bailey eyed her expectantly.

"Fine Bailey, I'll see what I can do. Since you're going to throw the best friend card and shit."

"Thank you. I love you too," she smiled.

"Anyway, you can save the mushy stuff. Let's get back to Marcus."

"What about him?" Bailey knitted her brows in confusion.

"Are you two officially a couple now?"

"Maybe after this is all over we can revisit the couple thing, but I don't know right now. I'm still—"

"Scared of loving him." Parker asked with a raised eyebrow.

"No its not—"

"Oh yes the hell it is. You're scared and you're trying to make sure that he's not messing around with Trina or Sabrina... or any other woman for that matter. I know you. Shit, I would be doing the same thing if I was about to put my heart on the line again. And that's okay for now, but you can't keep that man waiting like that. And you don't want to lose him Bailey, because honey from the look in your eyes, he's the one. Marcus is that one man that your heart won't be able to live without."

Chapter 29

Marcus pulled into the only available parking spot three houses up from Jeremy's house on the packed block and cut his engine. As he sat behind his steering wheel, Marcus carefully went over his approach to hopefully scare Jeremy into leaving Bailey alone, and getting him to take his hand out of this plot to help Trina blackmail him and Bailey. He'd never met two more pathetic people who actually wanted to blackmail people into having sex with them. Marcus hoped that a threat or two would make him back off, but if that didn't work, he was going make sure that two hungry pit bulls were waiting on him when he climbed into his car the next morning.

He opened his door and got ready to hop out of his truck when he saw Jeremy's porch light suddenly went dark. Thinking nothing of it at first, Marcus hopped out of his truck and started up the sidewalk when he saw the door open. Swiftly, Marcus ran and hid behind the tree in his neighbor's yard and carefully peeked around it.

"Well, well, well. What have we here? I knew there was a reason I didn't like your shady ass."

Marcus shook his head as Jeremy grabbed his brother's wife in a tongue kiss, while he palmed her ass and yanked her against his crotch. Snatching his phone from his pocket, he captured the moment several times before they shared another quick peck and she ran off to get in her car.

"Guess you won't be dog food by morning after all, you lucky son of a bitch." Marcus waited until she drove off before he merged into traffic.

"Y'all want ready to play dirty? Then let's play bitches."

******

Bailey cracked open her front door as soon as she heard Marcus pull up into her driveway and went back into her kitchen to finish browsing her carryout menus. Walking inside, he closed the door behind him.

"Bailey?"

"In here."

"Hey, what are you up to gorgeous?"

"I'm about to order some carryout from somewhere. I just haven't made my mind about what the heck I want," she said, browsing the take out menus that she kept on the side of the fridge.

"If you want, I can whip up something for you right quick."

"No Marcus, you've been running all day after work. Matter of fact, have you even eaten yet?" She turned to him and asked.

This man is just too fine...I want him to put me on this counter, lick chocolate off my tits and pussy, and then screw me until I'm coming all over the place.

"No but I was just about to—"

"Marcus, stop the excuses." She held her hand up, then placed her index finger to her lips. "Now, do you want to come help me pick a carryout, or do you want to go eat out?"Pulling her to him, Marcus smiled, kissed her on the lips, then spoke.

"I want whatever has you on the menu. Because the only thing I'm hungry for right now is you, woman." He pulled her close.

"While I definitely have no objections to that, it'll have to be after we've had some actual food."

"Fine. Let's go grab some barbeque."

"Now that sounds like a real plan right there. Let's go."

"Cool. Oh, before I forget we're going to break into Trina's house tomorrow night and hopefully we find some dirt on her."

"Wait what? We're going to do what? Break in to Trina's house?"

"It's the only way, Bailey."

"Oh no. Hell no. I am not breaking in to someone's house. It ain't happening. So you better come up with another plan." She moved around him and walked off toward her room.

"Bailey—"

"No Marcus, don't Bailey me. It's not happening Marcus and I mean it."

"Baby, it's the only way. This is the only chance we have." He grabbed her and tried to make her see reason.

"Maybe not. I got some things in motion. I'll know something in a day or two," she ran a hand through her hair, closed her eyes, and tried her best to keep it together.

"Some things in motion like what? I told you that I would take care of this Bailey. For both of us."

"I know Marcus, but I needed to do something too. I have to make my voice heard too. I can't just sit back and let you take care of everything. That's not my style. And it's only as back up or an option just in case we don't have a better plan."

"I understand. But would you have still went and looked for a backup if I was your man, your protector? Or would you had trusted me to take care of things?"

"I guess I would've trusted you to handle it but I—"

"Okay, fine. But Bailey listen, you know how much I care about you. That I want to be with you. That I want to be your man and protector, so sometimes I get a little ahead of myself but I mean everything I say. Maybe you don't trust me or maybe you just don't want me doing the things for you where it feels like I'm your man, but I enjoy those things no matter the obstacle. I know I can't make a decision for you nor would I ever want to, but I don't want to waste my time either; going back and forth with you when you have no intention other than keeping me as a friend. So tell me, will I always be nothing more than a friend?"

"Marcus I really can't—"

"Stop Bailey, just stop. Forget about it. I'll be downstairs if you need me."

"What about the barbeque?"

"Let me know when you're ready. I'll still go with you, but I'm okay. I'm not hungry anymore."

****

When Bailey woke up the next morning, she was so emotionally drained that she didn't want to get out of bed but the feeling was temporarily overshadowed by the delicious smell of bacon, French toast, and omelets. Rising from her bed, she cleaned herself up and let her nose guide her to the food.

"Good morning Bailey. I made you breakfast." Marcus gave a warm smile as Bailey entered the kitchen.

"Morning. Thank you so much."

"You're welcome. There's fresh OJ in the fridge. And all of the food is on the stove."

"Oh all right, you're not eating with me?"

"No, I have errands to run and I think it's best that I start giving you some space. I only cooked breakfast because you fell asleep last night without eating your dinner."

"Marcus I—"

"Bailey, let's leave yesterday in the past." He glanced down at his wristwatch, downed his glass of orange juice, and grabbed a piece of bacon.

"I got to get going. I'll talk to you later. And just to warn you, I'm breaking into Trina's house tonight. With or without you. If you want to tag along call me by ten and I'll pick you up, unless you want to drive yourself, which is cool. Either way, just let me know something."

"Marcus, I don't want-I'm just—"

"Bye Bailey." Marcus grabbed up his phone and walked out the door.

"...scared. I'm scared of loving you. I just want you to understand. I need for you to understand and be patient with me. I love you," Bailey whispered as a single tear slid down her cheek.

Chapter 30

Marcus could've stayed and had breakfast with Bailey, but he was tired of her bullshit. He wanted to wait on her to get her damn feelings together, but he felt like he'd given her more than enough time, and the last thing he was going to do was hound or beg anyone to be with him. He'd given Bailey numerous chances to figure herself out, and he was tired. He'd never been so mentally annoyed at something in his whole life.

Shit, she either wants to be with me or she doesn't. And from the looks of things, friends are all we'll ever be. And I have to accept that. Hell, I am going to accept that. I'm done waiting on her to figure out this and figure out that. It ain't that much damn figuring in the world. So I'm done playing around with her. And I'm serious this time. There's nothing else to talk about. If we're friends then that's it—we're friends. I'm accepting it and moving on. That shit is over.

Turning down Anthony's block, he pulled up and honked his horn. A few minutes later, his friend came running out the door.

"Hey bro, I see that you ready for that ass whopping early today huh?"

"Dude when have you ever whipped me in basketball?"

"A few times," Marcus laughed.

"Right, a few times."

"Five or six to twenty ain't nothing to brag about, Ant," Marcus chuckled.

"Man whatever, just save the trash talking for the court."

"Oh you know it's coming. Did you call Jeremy?"

"Nope. Why not?" Anthony asked with a raised eyebrow.

"Your boy is foul. I've been telling you that from day one."

"Marcus, seriously what he do now?"

"You mean other than blackmailing Bailey to screw her and screwing his brother's wife?"

"Marcus, quit lying bro. I know you don't really care for him but—"

"Anthony, I can prove it. This is serious."

"I go out of town for a few weeks and shit turns upside down. Man. What happened?" When Marcus relayed the story, Anthony couldn't believe it.

"Marcus, that shit is way past foul. I didn't believe you before, but I definitely believe you now. He's been blowing me off lately too. I guess I know why now."

"I tried to tell you something wasn't right about him. But I bet you after tomorrow, he won't do this to anybody else."

"I hear you. It sounds like you got everything under control, but let me know if you need help taking that clown down. I can't wait to get ahold of him. It's going to be an all-out brawl when or if I ever see

Jeremy again. I think he knows by now that I know he's a snake."

"Yup. I agree. I'll bet money on it."

"I never saw this coming. He was such a good dude. But what I want to know is what's up with you and Bailey?"

"Nothing. And I'm done chasing her. Last night was the last straw. She wants to be friends and that's it."

"So you're just going to give up Marcus?"

"Yeah, there's nothing else I can do," he shrugged.

"I never took you for a quitter, Marcus. And when I think about it, you've never quit anything in your life. I say keep fighting. She's definitely worth it."

"Keep fighting for what, Anthony? To look like an ass? While she's out here searching for the man she wants to be. What sense does that make?"

"I'm just saying, I think you should try harder. I really think she's the one for you. And you know that says a lot coming from me, because I don't believe in all that love shit. But you and Bailey, that's real. That's divine. So keep fighting Marcus, don't be stupid. I wouldn't let that one get away if I were you."

"I would've agreed with you had I seen that my efforts were going somewhere but Anthony, Bailey can't even answer a simple question about us. So I'm just throwing in the towel. Bailey doesn't want me and for the first time the feeling may be mutual."

"Marcus, quit being a punk and learn to have some patience. Be patient with her, that kind of love that you two have for each other is worth going through hell and back for if need be. Remember that Marcus. Write that shit don't, so you never forget it.

*****

"Bailey, calm down. Everything is going to be all right," Marcus tried to calm Bailey as he parked at the end of Trina's block.

"You mean just like it was when you talked me into watching your little peepshow and we almost got arrested?" she sarcastically cupped her hand to her ear and waited for a response.

"That was just a minor miscalculation on my part," he laughed.

"Right. If you say so," Bailey chuckled.

"You said you trusted me the other day, so trust me. We're going to be in and out. Twenty minutes tops. This is going to be a piece of cake. All right?"

"This is going to be a disaster, but I guess I'm in."

"That's good enough for me. Now let's go," he opened his car door.

"Wait Marcus, I need to tell you something."

"Bailey, can't you tell me later? We have to—"

"I love you. I mean, I'm scared of loving you because I'm afraid of getting hurt. But I'm so in love with you and I love you so much. I'm afraid of trying and failing again. I'm afraid of getting my heart broken. I fear falling in love with you. But I've fallen and I'm finding out that it's not so bad. It's rather nice actually. You make me feel things and do things that I only read about. It feels so unreal when we're together. But I love it. I love every minute of it. I don't want to lose it. I don't want to lose you. I love you, but I'm so scared. But if you could be patient with me and wouldn't mind taking things slow, I would love for you to be my protector, my friend, and the love of my life," Bailey finished with tears in her eyes. Reaching into the center console, Marcus grabbed a couple of Kleenex and wiped the big crocodile tears that were running splashing down her cheeks.

"Bailey, I'm scared too but I swear I've never wanted to risk my heart so bad for any woman other than you."

Grabbing her into his arms, Marcus wrapped his arms around Bailey and held her as if his last breath depended on it. He took a deep breath and slowly let her go, then he moved back in for a long, lingering slow kiss with plenty of tongue, and a peek of what was to come later on that night.

"Thank you for taking a chance on me beautiful."

"Thanks for waiting, handsome."

"You ready to put an end to this madness?"

"Absolutely."

"Then let's go."

Once Marcus gave Bailey the okay after checking to make sure the coast was clear, they scurried down the street until they reached Trina's house. Going around back, Marcus picked the back door lock and within seconds, they were in. Bailey quietly closed the door behind them

"Why doesn't she have an alarm on her house in this neighborhood?" Bailey asked.

"I don't know, but works out better for us because she doesn't have one."

"She doesn't have any dogs, does she?" Bailey stopped dead in her tracks and listened while scanning the room with her flashlight.

"Not that I know of."

"What the hell do you mean not that you know of?" Bailey frowned. "Weren't you supposed to check that out and any other parameters before you decided to break in?"

"Bailey damn it, we're fine. Now let's stop arguing, split up, look for something to expose Trina, and get the hell out of here."

"We are not splitting up. I don't know what you think this is, but you know what happens every single time people split up; especially black people."

"Bailey, you watch too much television and too many damn scary movies," Marcus laughed.

"Laugh all you want, but you know I'm right."

"Whatever you say baby. Let's just go find her bedroom or and office."

"Lead the way." They made their way down a long hallway until they came to the first door on the left. Bingo. The bedroom.

"Search the drawers Bailey. I'll check the closet." They split and began franticly searching. Two minutes later, Bailey joined Marcus in the closet.

"I found nothing but a few forged checks and a huge porno selection. What about you Marcus?"

"More porn, whips, chains, and an escort service she uses frequently. A bunch of sex toys, but nothing to nail her on."

"Okay, well I'll check the next room," Bailey headed to the door.

"What happened to not splitting up, scary ass?" Marcus chuckled.

"I'm going to try and be brave this time." Bailey exited the room, and not a minute later she raced back to Marcus just as he was coming out.

"Bailey what's wrong?" Marcus wrinkled his face in confusion.

"I heard something," Bailey whispered as she clung on tight to him.

"Bailey, you just left the room. How did you hear something that quick?"

"I don't know, but I did. Let's just go. This is starting to creep me out."

"Bailey just a few more—"

Marcus' sentence was cut short when they both heard a loud bang, and then what sounded like someone trying to open the front door.

"Seeeeeeee, I told you that I heard something. We're going to jail. We're fucking going to prison," Bailey whispered with fear in her eyes.

"Baby no we're not. Go now. Run. In the closet."

Bailey took off, and Marcus was fast on her heels. Because the walk-in closet was so big, they were able to hide behind storage bins and in between clothes and not be seen with the door opened, but if whoever it was at the door began searching, all hell was going to break loose. Placing his index finger to his lips as beads of sweat began to spout out from his body, he signaled across the closet for Bailey to stay quiet as the front door came crashing open, and footsteps soon padded softy down the hall. Wide-eyed, Bailey slapped both hands over her mouth and prayed that she didn't scream from nervousness.

"Shit. I need a drink!" Trina yelled as she dragged her suitcase into her bedroom and turned on the light. "What a day. What a long ass damn day. But I'm more than happy to be back home." Trina pulled her hair up into a ponytail and started to undress. She was getting ready to step into her nightgown when they front door opened and closed again.

"Honey I'm home," Jeremy laughed as he shut the door behind him and ambled his way down the hall.

Rushing to her bedroom door in nothing but a smile, Trina was greeted by Jeremy with a huge grin as he picked her up and carried her over to the bed. He laid her down and quickly began to undress. With their eyes now the size of silver dollars from shock, Bailey and Marcus both locked eyes, then Bailey quickly snatched her cell from her pocket and tossed it to Marcus since he was closest to the door for him to record them.

"Did everything go according to plan while I was away?"

"Sure did, those two idiots are running scared."

"Good. Just the way I want it."

"I can't believe that we're really getting away with this."

"I just knew Marcus would ask for the tape that I don't even have. Ha! We blackmailed their ass with nothing but a straight face and a threat."

"Yes we did. But baby let's talk about that later. The only thing I want to do is hear you scream my name while I slide in your pussy. Now open up for daddy baby."

"Yes daddy. But only if you take me against the shower wall, like you did last week," Trina giggled as she spread her legs.

"I'll do anything you want me to do, baby."

Chapter 31

Marcus hadn't felt this good in a long time. Things were starting to look up. A sly smirk slid across his lips as he strode into to work. Walking toward his office, he greeted his coworkers with utter excitement.

Today is going to be a good day.

Once in his office, he put away his things and got right down to work. Because he was so busy, he'd worked right through lunch and only noticed when his stomach began growling at him. After making a few calls, Marcus pushed back from his desk and decided to go head out to check to see what was being served in the cafeteria for lunch, when he opened his door to Trina posted against the door frame with a big Cheshire cat grin.

"Hello sexy."

"Trina excuse me, I have—"

"Oh no Marcus, you will not just dismiss me. We have some unfinished business to tend to and you know it. Now why don't you just back up and move out of my way before you piss—"

"Marcus. A moment of your time now," their boss Maxwell Rogers interrupted them and signaled for Marcus from just outside of his office door. Marcus looked from Rogers's door back to Trina.

Why does he want to see me? Did she already leak the tape? Was yesterday a set up? Did Trina know that Bailey and I were in her home yesterday? Did we leave something behind?

"Don't look at me, I have no idea what he wants," Trina's smirk said an entirely different story.

"Move. Now," Marcus spoke in a deathly low tone.

"Be careful how you speak to me, Marcus," Trina stepped aside and let him through.

Marcus disappeared into Maxwell's office, and Trina waited until he came out thirty minutes later. Seeming distraught, Marcus headed back to his office, and Trina smiled as she leaned against the wall. Strolling into his office, he pushed the door closed behind him, but immediately turned around when he didn't hear it click shut.

"So what was that all about?" Trina strutted inside, and closed and locked the door.

"Trina, now is not a good time. So Back off."

"Listen I'm not going anywhere until I come damn it. So stop fucking playing around and let's get to fucking business. Pun intended," she winked.

"Or what Trina, you're going to go running to Maxwell and headquarters and give them the tape of me and Bailey fucking? Well go ahead. Do it. Bye."

"Marcus sweetie, now is not the time to call my bluff," she smiled thinly.

"Who says I'm bluffing Trina? Go. Tell. I dare you."

"Fine. You will regret this Marcus."

"No I won't. And while you're at it, make sure you explain to them how your sex tape starring you and Jeremy last night was sent to the corporate email, along with text messages and emails about how you've been blackmailing men at work to have sex with you. And how you've been stealing money to pay for you little sex fetishes." Stopping dead in her track, Trina slowly turned around. She suddenly looked deathly ill.

"You broke into my house and hacked into my computer and phone?"

"Prove it."

Trina sneered at him, but held her tongue.

"Didn't think so."

"This isn't over," Trina stormed toward the door.

"Oh but it is. So on your way out of the office today, take everything with you because you're fired. And do me a favor and stop by your friend Jeremy's desk and take that sick ass bastard with you."

"Ha! Sweetheart, you can't fire me. Are you drunk?" she laughed hysterically.

"Wrong again, because as the new VP of Unveil Magazine, I can do anything I want. So am I drunk you say, yes, I sure am... with power. Now get the fuck out of my office."

******

Bailey gulped down her second glass of wine as she sat on the edge of her couch, nervously bouncing her leg up and down awaiting the outcome of what happened when Marcus turned the tables on Trina, when he came strolling in the house.

"What happened? How did it go? Was she pissed?" Bailey jumped up and asked excitedly.

"She was livid," Marcus walked up to Bailey and kissed her softly on the lips.

"Yes!" Bailey celebrated by throwing her fist in the air and rooting for the home team.

"Bet she'll think again before she tries that mess with anyone else. I still say we should've leaked that tape and got them both fired."

"Funny you should mention that. I was promoted to VP today because Max wants to retire, have his son and run the company. So, as my first order of business, I took the motherfuckin' trash out, baby."

"What? Oh my God. You're serious. Baby I'm so happy for you. And that Trina got exactly what she deserved."

"Not just Trina, Jeremy's slick ass too."

"Oh yeah, we bad." Bailey jumped up and did a victory dance, then planted a big fat kiss on Marcus' cheek. "I'm so sorry I doubted you Marcus."

"No worries baby. I never mind proving my love for you."

"So if I ask you a question, to prove your love, you'd answer it honesty?" she eyed him skeptically.

"Yeah, but I'm getting the feeling you're trying to ask me something, so spit it out," he laughed.

"Well, I saw you sitting with the owner of The Orange Slice and—"

"Her grandmother had passed away and she just confided in me. No, nothing is going on between us. She wanted to get to know me better, but I told her I wanted you. You're the only one who holds my heart. You have nothing to worry about, Bailey."

"Oh I know I didn't, but I was checking to make sure that you were the one who had nothing to worry about," she tapped his chin before walking off to the den.

"You're something else woman. Come here." Marcus pulled Bailey into his arms and planted sweet kisses along her neck.

"Bailey, let me tell you something, I love you more than life itself. You'll never have to wonder or question your position in my life, because you will always know. And one day real soon, I'm going to marry you and then we're going to have some beautiful babies together. In you, I really think I found the love of my life. And yes those are the lyrics to Jazmine Sullivan's *Let it Burn*; that's exactly how you make me feel. I'm going to do everything in my power to make sure I give you more reasons to smile than frown. I love you. I love your soul. And I'm going to spend the rest of my life, showing you just how much."

With tears running down her cheeks, Bailey leaned in and kissed Marcus gently on the lips before resting her head on his chest.

"I love you too, Marcus Alexander. More than you'll ever know."

"I know baby, I know. Now let's go finish celebrating, I brought new ties," he winked suggestively.

"Okay, but you're going to have to be very careful because I don't want us to hurt the baby."

"Baby, I can be as gentle and as rough–hold on, did you—baby? We're having a baby? Bailey, are you pregnant with my child."

"Yup, I sure am," she giggled.

"Oh my God." Marcus grabbed her up off the floor and carried her toward the bedroom as he planted kisses all over her face.

"I'm scared Marcus. I'm so scared," Bailey whispered as he carefully placed her in the center of the bed, and began to undress her.

"I'm scared too baby. I'm scared too." Marcus quickly undressed and climbed on top of Bailey, gently burying himself inside of her wet warmth.

"But as your protector, friend, and the love of your life, I have a feeling that everything is going to be just fine." He added, allowing himself to become lost in her sweet nectar.

Stay in touch with the author

Facebook:

India T. Norfleet

Thanks so much for supporting our journey. To stay up-to-date on future novels, contests, and giveaways text daniellemarcus to 22828

Or

Join our Danielle Marcus Presents Reading Group on Facebook. We'd love to kick it with the people that support us.

Email: Daniellemarcuspresents@yahoo.com

0566681605

CPSIA information can be obtained
at www.ICGtesting.com
Printed in the USA
LVOW10s1605310317
529202LV00009B/544/P